'I want you, you know that,' Ethan breathed harshly. 'You feel the same. For pity's sake, we hardly know each other! Why?'

Flustered, Roxy tried to pull away from the magnetic field that pulled them inexorably to one another. She didn't like losing control, ever.

'Mass outbreak in hormones, I suppose,' she croaked.

He glared. 'Don't try to escape me,' he said softly. 'I'm not allowing this to affect me forever. I don't like it. I'll get you out of my system soon. Divert me with humour if you wish; you'll still end up where I want you.' His eyes glowed with a primeval hunger. 'Beneath me. Naked and hungry,' he whispered starkly.

Books you will enjoy
by SARA WOOD

LOVE NOT DISHONOUR

Judging from her desperate plea, Lucy's half-sister Selina was the innocent victim of the arrogant Max Mazzardi's cruel nature. But when Lucy arrived in beautiful Lake Maggiore to help Selina, she found a very different situation. Worse, she was drawn to the very man she detested...

MASTER OF CASHEL

Caitlin resented Jake Ferriter for taking her beloved home, Cashelkerry, and blamed him for causing her father's death. But she could not deny the attraction she felt for this enigmatic, ruthless man. The feeling was mutual—but could she cope with his offer of an affair without commitment?

THREAT OF POSSESSION

BY
SARA WOOD

MILLS & BOON LIMITED
ETON HOUSE   18-24 PARADISE ROAD
RICHMOND   SURREY   TW9 1SR

First published in Great Britain 1989
by Mills & Boon Limited

© Sara Wood 1989

Australian copyright 1989
Philippine copyright 1990
This edition 1990

ISBN 0 263 76528 8

Set in Times Roman 10½ on 11½ pt.
01-9001-53417 C

Made and printed in Great Britain

CHAPTER ONE

ROXY PAGE swept into her Oxford Street shop, accompanied by the sharp staccato of her five-inch heels and an aroma of Paradise. Scattering 'good mornings' on either side to the staff, she stopped only briefly to rearrange a display before running up a broad flight of stairs to the suite of offices.

'Morning, Joe.' Roxy grinned at her secretary and threw her scarlet Homburg hat on to a black leather sofa, shaking her mop of tousled, jet-black hair that had taken ages to disarray to her satisfaction. 'Isn't it a fabulous day?'

'Hmm. You're in one of *those* moods, are you? It's the end of March, cold, the sky is grey——'

'Oh, that,' she dismissed with a wave of her expressive hands, which seemed to be constantly in motion. 'I feel on top of the world. So should you. After lunch I'll be planning two more "Zest!" shops.'

Joe eyed her doubtfully. 'You don't have the finance yet—— '

'Of course I have!' she cried in astonishment, sky-blue eyes bright with excitement. 'Just as soon as I've gnawed my way through a lamb chop and explained what a sure-fire success we're going to be. How could anyone *not* lend me money?'

Joe's doubts melted visibly away. She exuded total confidence in herself and it was catching. No one could resist Roxy when she was brimming with enthusiasm. He was already feeling as if he'd been infused with energy just by her presence in the room.

'Poor man,' he said, with a sigh, thinking of her unsuspecting lunch date. 'I'm half inclined to ring this financier up and warn him that he's having lunch with a Lorelei. You'd lure any man on to the rocks given half a chance, especially when you're feeling bouncy, like today.'

'Investing in my business is a certainty,' she said firmly. 'Any idiot can see that.'

'Some of your suppliers are putting a spoke in your wheel. We'll have to watch them if you want to keep your reputation for efficiency,' said Joe. 'We're having problems again.'

'Oh, lord.' Roxy poured herself a cup of black coffee and lifted the fine bone china to her poppy-coloured lips. 'Let me get my shot of caffeine and take my coat off first.'

The cup was quickly drained, the magenta jacket was flung to the couch and she strode over to Joe's desk, placing her fingers together in an attitude of prayer.

'Deliver me from non-delivery,' she begged irreverently.

Joe smiled. She was an extraordinary combination of waif and sophisticate, of organisation and chaos. Sometimes he felt old and staid beside her; sometimes her brain moved so fast and at such odd—but brilliant—tangents, that he was left standing. Whereas most people thought things through carefully, Roxy had the ability to make an immediate decision and stick with it, almost forcing it to work by sheer grit and personality alone.

He'd been with Roxy for two years now, ever since she'd expanded one dingy little health food shop into a vibrant chain of outlets that exported all over the world. She alone vitalised her staff and the very atmosphere of each shop with her particular brand of enthusiasm and optimism.

In a remarkably short time, she'd revamped everything and everyone who worked for her, and every day had been fast, furious and fun. And often frantic, as they all tried to keep up with her sudden changes of plan. Roxy's instant decisions were famous—or perhaps infamous.

'Fresh herbs. Can't get them,' he said crisply. Roxy didn't like long-winded explanations. She darted from one point to another too quickly to get involved in detail.

Roxy made a face and picked up a phone, jabbing at the numbers with the stub of a pencil. One of her hands rested on a slender hip belligerently and her eyes glinted, happy at the challenge.

'Charlie,' she said in a matter-of-fact tone, 'I'm in awful trouble. Be an angel and pop down to Dorset. Have a word with Miss Williams...get supplies going... Sure, but you're so good at the personal touch. You're the only one I can ask who has any chance of succeeding... Thanks! Ring me when you have any news.'

Her high forehead creased as she put the phone down. 'Get on to the shops, Joe. Warn them. *Darnation!*'

'They're only a tiny part of our sales,' he said, trying to get a sense of proportion.

She flashed him a sharp look. 'That's not the point,' she said in rebuke. 'If I offer fresh herbs for sale, that's what the customer gets. Perfection, Joe. I won't accept anything less.'

Her mouth tight with determination, she stalked into her own room. That was the third time supplies had come to a halt for one reason or another. *Why* didn't matter to her, only the end result: that her well-run organisation faltered. Roxy couldn't accept that. She'd put all her energies into establishing the most favoured health food shops in London, and had succeeded because she wouldn't compromise, would never accept second-best, would never admit defeat, instead using her assertiveness to badger, coax or charm people into giving way.

She stopped and flicked a proud glance around her ultra-modern, high-tech office in her favourite colours of black, white and flame. Roxy's slim wool dress—a simple and expensive Ungaro—was in a startling orange, a wide black belt cinching in her tiny waist. An assortment of huge black jet beads weighed down her slender throat and she'd tied an Indian shawl, in shades of crimson and fuchsia, around her curvy hips.

The effect, with her dramatic colouring, was stunning. Beautifully groomed, the envy of all who knew her and the object of men's desire, Roxy had everything she'd ever wanted: success, power and a stimulating life. She and London went together. The city buzzed, hummed, vibrated in tune with her, changing constantly, as she did, offering variety and excitement. Yet there always seemed to be one more mountain to climb; contentment eluded her. Although she wasn't sure she wanted it.

The same went for romance. Experience had told her that a lover expected to be dominant in everything. Roxy had been 'her own woman' for so long that she couldn't bear to be dictated to. She had no intention of fitting into a man's idea of what his perfect woman should do, and how she ought to behave. She sighed. It was a pity men were initially attracted to her independence and lively personality, then tried to domesticate her!

She'd held out against acting the slave for a man. Domesticity had no appeal. She'd had two long-term relationships and, when the initial infatuation had died down, she'd tried loyally to evoke some deep feelings from within, but had failed. She was beginning to think that there was some truth in the popular assessment of the Gemini personality. Roxy's eyes grew troubled. Beneath her darting, butterfly nature there might be a darting butterfly, incapable of any emotional commitment.

But for the moment, at least, her lack of ties was an advantage. It meant she devoted all her considerable energies to the business. And that world was far more exciting to her than being pawed after a boring evening.

It puzzled her that she could be so unlike her mother in temperament. Roxy's mobile face grew thoughtful, and her eyes clouded as they dropped to the photograph on her desk. In the privacy of her office, she stood silent and still as grief stole into her heart. That sorrow stayed totally contained, though; she hadn't yet cried one tear since hearing the news of her mother's death.

She picked up the silver-framed photograph, studying her mother's homely face, and a wave of loneliness washed over her.

I miss you. You're the only one who knows who I am, inside. Now there's no one, no one at all.

Roxy's eyes glazed. She put down the photo and fought to control the choking sensation in her throat. Only three months ago, she'd heard that her mother had perished in an accidental fire. It was little comfort that there would have been no pain, that she'd suffocated in her sleep from the smoke which had damaged one wing of the house where she worked as a housekeeper. But Roxy still agonised over the scene she had conjured up in her mind, imagining the flames and billowing black smoke.

Her mother had worked for old Mrs Tremaine, an eccentric recluse who forbade visitors, so she hadn't seen the house. It was in Cornwall, anyway. Still, her mother had described it in her letters, and chattered about it on the few occasions she'd been able to get away from the bedridden old lady long enough to meet her daughter. It was a vast house for two people, far too much for her mother to manage, since she acted as Mrs Tremaine's nurse as well. And, without a gardener's care, the grounds were slowly becoming overgrown, like Sleeping Beauty's garden.

Two women, living alone, dying alone. How awful. And Mrs Tremaine's son and daughter were on the neighbouring land, a barrier of hatred between them. That was bizarre.

Roxy's sad eyes grew hard. At the funeral in December, Ethan Tremaine had done nothing to welcome her or to show compassion. Yet he had made a far greater impact on her than she could have imagined. Used to attracting people, Roxy had been affronted that Ethan ignored her. Although, she mused, he'd been unaware of everyone. It was as if no one else existed and he was totally alone.

Her brows knitted together. That was the umpteenth time since the funeral that she'd caught herself thinking about Ethan, instead of getting on with her life. But then, he was a very enigmatic man.

The phones in her office began to go like crazy, and messages came through on her fax machine. Roxy allowed herself a wry and wistful sigh, then switched into high gear once more.

In the middle of a peaceful lull, during which she began to check the proposed launch for a new shop in Bristol, Roxy was interrupted by her intercom.

'Yes, Joe?' she called. Her quick eye spotted a flaw in the shop's layout and deftly improved on it.

'There's an Ethan Tremaine on the line.'

Roxy felt her chin rise aggressively, and smiled wryly at her instinctive reaction.

'Never heard of him,' she said with satisfaction.

With a quirk of her brightly painted lips, she bent to work on the plans again. After pumping cold hostility into her direction after one brief glance of his cold, green eyes, then virtually ignoring her at the funeral, he needn't think he could imperiously call her up whenever he wanted to. She was busy.

Joe buzzed again. 'He says, "The hell she has," and he's damned if he'll be fobbed off by your live-in lover.' He sounded curious. 'How did he get hold of your personal number? And who is this guy?'

'A descendant of Attila the Hun,' she joked. 'Tell him I'm ironing my apron.'

'What?'

'You heard.' Roxy giggled.

As Roxy had approached the village church where her mother and Mrs Tremaine were due to be buried, Ethan's sister had sneeringly announced that the housekeeper's daughter had arrived. Ethan had barely bothered to turn his head, but Annabel had tugged his sleeve, whispering. That was when his hard, unfeeling eyes had run over Roxy's outfit, bypassing her face as they registered astonishment. And no wonder! Not many females wore ancient raincoats and caps to funerals!

Of course, if the Tremaines had been vaguely polite, she would have explained her extraordinary dress and made sure they'd seen the elegant black suit beneath. As it was, their supercilious attitude meant that she didn't give a damn what they thought.

She had found it hard enough keeping the tears back, without waltzing up to the arrogant Ethan and watching him look down his nose at her while she made excuses for herself. It would have taken only a few sneering words from him to make her burst into a torrent of tears, and she was darned if she'd do that in front of him.

Roxy's mother had always been sensitive about being a housekeeper, and Roxy was aware of her embarrassment from an early age. So she'd become quick to get riled when anyone sneered. It had offended her that the stigma rose again at her mother's funeral. It seemed Ethan found it distasteful to be sharing a graveside with a servant's daughter. He was an incredible snob, she thought, stabbing viciously with her pencil at an inoffensive paper-clip.

'Roxy?'

'Now what?' she muttered in irritation.

She realised crossly that Ethan wouldn't take no for an answer. In fact, she doubted that anyone ever denied him anything. He had that arrogant contempt of a well-fed cat who knew how to make people run around in circles after him. She smiled. Not this cookie! How lovely, to get her own back by denying his existence!

'My ear hurts,' complained Joe.

'Go on,' Roxy sighed.

'He yelled,' said Joe irritably. 'He snarled something about you being bloody-minded, and would I impress on your evidently feckless mind that he had something important to say?'

'OK. Put him through,' she said, taking pity on Joe—but not on the obnoxious Ethan. She had an idea. A wicked idea.

'Yeah? 'Ullo?' she cried, in a grating Cockney accent. That ought to be housekeeper-like enough for him!

'Roxanne? This is Roxanne Page? My solicitor gave me this number——'

It was a low, gravelly voice that made Roxy's toes curl a little. 'Yeah. What d'ya want?' She chewed an imaginary piece of gum as she spoke, and made her own voice coarser in contrast to his.

'I'd like to talk to you,' he husked, making the line vibrate in her ear.

Seductive devil. 'Not interested,' she said, lying. She was *fascinated*!

'Please have the good manners to hear me out,' he said grimly, sounding as if he were ninety-four. Stuffy stick-in-the-mud, thought Roxy. 'I have a proposition to make.'

'A prop position? Are you being cheeky? That sounds rude to me. Is this one of them 'eavy breathin' phone calls?' she accused, taking a delight in teasing him out of his solemnity.

She heard Ethan swear softly, then speak slowly, obviously choosing his words with care, as if he thought she was stupid.

'No, Roxanne, it isn't. You know who I am. Your late mother was my mother's servant.'

He put a slight emphasis on the word 'servant', and Roxanne bristled, feeling even more inclined to disconcert him. Did he expect her to curtsy or something? She remembered vividly how his sister Annabel, as skinny and neat as a dainty bird, had muttered the word 'common' as Roxy slid into the pew opposite. That had upset her too, intensifying her low opinion of the haughty Tremaines.

'That don't give you no right to say no rude things,' she said petulantly, enjoying herself hugely and getting a little muddled with the number of times she could put 'no' into a sentence.

He sighed heavily. 'I'm not. You've made a mistake. Can I meet you for tea somewhere? I want to make you an offer——'

'Ooooh, Mr Tremaine! You are wicked!' she screamed, relishing his gasp as her high-pitched squawk rang down the line and pierced his eardrum. 'I'll tell me bloke about you!'

'Now, listen, it's nothing like that. I only want——'

'I know what you want,' she said vigorously, going slightly over the top as usual. Roxy could never leave well alone. 'All you gen'lemen is the same. Servants ain't safe from the likes of you.'

'Are you having me on?' he asked suspiciously.

'The very idea!' she cried indignantly, trying hard not to laugh.

'Roxanne, it's very important that you pay attention,' he said in exasperation. 'Give me an hour of your time and you might walk away able to live in comfort.'

'I knew it! Blue movies! Funny positions, like what you said. You saucy devil!' she breathed.

'Oh, for Pete's sake!' he roared, and slammed the phone down.

Joe hurried in at the sound of Roxy's peals of laughter, grinning with relief when he saw she wasn't being hysterical.

'Oh, Joe, I haven't laughed so much for ages,' she cried weakly. 'Good old Ethan. He's contributed something to my well-being at last.'

'Then you're available if he rings again?' asked Joe mildly.

'No,' she sighed, wiping her eyes and checking her mascara. 'Tell him you'll thump him if he rings your bird again and makes improper suggestions about positions and payment for them.'

Joe smiled. He'd carried some odd messages from her to various men friends, and this was by no means the oddest.

'Do I get any benefits from pretending to be your lover?' he asked hopefully.

'Don't ruin a lovely friendship,' grinned Roxy. 'Back to the slave galley and row like mad. We've got a ship to run.'

Laughing, Joe returned to his office, leaving her to wonder idly why Ethan had telephoned. But she didn't really care. Nothing he did was of any interest to her at all.

That wasn't strictly true, she thought ruefully, acknowledging that she was deceiving herself. Since the funeral she'd found herself thinking about him often, and she wondered why he should fascinate her so much. Certainly she'd been unduly annoyed by Ethan's extraordinary behaviour. She knew he'd been estranged from his mother, and was a cold fish, but she hadn't expected to be so completely snubbed. Nor had she been prepared for the impact he'd made on her curiosity, and on her senses.

The weather on that December day had been atrocious. Rain fell out of the sky in sheets and everyone there had cowered under umbrellas. Not Ethan. It had seemed as if he hardly noticed that his dark wavy hair was saturated and dripping on to the collar of his thick black wool coat. Like a rugged rock off the Cornish coast, his implacable face had lifted in proud contempt as the rain washed over its chiselled granite lines.

He wasn't conventionally handsome at all, his features too harsh and holding a threat of chilling menace. The dark brows remained lowered throughout the ceremony, the green eyes like a distant field.

Ethan's head and shoulders towered over them all, his back uncompromisingly broad, hands thrust deep into his pockets. Annabel's sulky clinging made as little impression on him as a fly on an ox's flank. An imperceptible twitch of his arm warned his sister not to bother him with her chatter. Roxy had felt almost sorry for the frail-looking woman, who seemed to rely on Ethan totally and was finding his remoteness upsetting.

He had spoken to no one, looked at no one, after that cursory glance in her direction. Roxy gained an impression of a man who was totally alone and had deliberately chosen that path in preference to any other. Ethan Tremaine gave out the appearance of being like a rocky island: emotionally immune to life and death, self-sufficient, contained.

She doubted much could touch his heart. It lay, she was sure, beating regularly beneath that big chest, never losing its rhythm for a moment. Women would come and go in his life, but Roxy felt they would never disturb his equilibrium.

Stern and aloof as it was, his appearance had haunted Roxy. She'd never seen anyone so remote and withdrawn before. It made her want to create some kind of an impact on him, to force him to acknowledge her existence as a human being. That his manner extended to all the mourners and officials didn't matter one jot. Roxy needed people to smile at her, to laugh, argue, get angry—anything, providing they reacted. Being shut out was a totally new and uncomfortable experience.

No wonder women were attracted to him, like suicidal moths. His enigmatic, brooding silence was a challenge! It was her mother who had told her of Ethan's exploits with women. It seemed incredible that he'd ever unbent sufficiently to encourage them, but Roxy had felt a strong sexual aura around him, despite the strong, silent act. But she suspected that it was a purely physical drive which he satisfied, with a callous ruthlessness, and that there was no room for tenderness.

The village seethed with gossip about the girls, and later the women, who had fallen for his magnetic good looks. Broken hearts lay scattered like discarded eggshells as Ethan steadfastly refused to be pinned down by any one of his girlfriends, however hard they tried.

Roxy paused in skimming through the day's mail. Ethan and his sister had never visited Mrs Tremaine, even when she was ill. Now they'd inherited that huge estate and would share the old lady's wealth. Whereas she only had a few photos of her mother and one or two trinkets. And precious few memories.

Finding her eyes moist, Roxy shut her mind to the past, seeing that she would become miserable if she dwelt on her loss. Many times her enviable capacity to discipline herself had prevented her emotions from distracting her. It was a delaying tactic, of course. One day she'd have to face up to her grief. But not yet. She had a demanding organisation to mastermind.

The day's business was dealt with briskly and Joe collected her dictation tapes and instructions. After a satisfying lunch with the financier who was interested in financing more 'Zest!' shops in Manchester and Leeds, Roxy celebrated by doing a little exclusive shopping, extravagantly purchasing more than she should because of the amount of champagne and happiness bubbling away in her bloodstream.

Laden with carrier bags, she leapt exuberantly into a taxi and arrived back at the office, very late, and riding high with elation. She'd cracked it! This was the beginning: nationwide chains of shops...a household name...freedom to do whatever she liked, unhampered by anyone else... Heaven!

In a happy blur, she whirled into the shop, only to stop in astonishment at the sight of the tall, dark man standing at one of the counters and glaring at one of her assistants.

The Cornish rock had come to London. Ethan Tremaine!

CHAPTER TWO

Roxy stared, thinking the champagne might be affecting her eyesight, but the man was unmistakable. He still stood out in the crowd, still seemed strangely contained amid the hectic bustle of the store.

Whatever was he doing here? And dressed in a very slick piece of suiting, too! She hadn't realised before how well he wore his clothes. Or, she mused, maybe anything would look good on that big, hunky body. He was certainly getting the full attention of the women browsing in the shop. The man must be used to having his vanity fed every time he climbed out of bed.

Slowly unbuttoning the magenta jacket in the warmth indoors, she paused, realising what he'd done. He'd come up from Cornwall that morning! He couldn't have had time to drive here after talking to her on the phone, he must have caught the train. Talk about persistent! Roxy's curiosity became intense. She was consumed with the need to know why he was so keen to see her—without appearing eager to know. She didn't want him to think she was the kind of woman who found him interesting.

'I don't believe she's not around,' he was saying stubbornly to the assistant, and leaning on the counter in an intimidating posture.

'Well, she isn't,' insisted the girl helplessly.

Roxy slid behind a display of vitamin pills and peered around its shelves. All she could see was Ethan's straddled legs, planted firmly and assertively.

'It's almost four o'clock. She can't still be at lunch.'

19

'It's not unusual.'

'I don't believe it!' he growled. 'No wonder businesses fold. Surely she's back?'

'I'm sorry, sir,' said the girl. 'She tends to make her own schedules.'

'Well, she wouldn't last long in my employ,' he muttered.

Roxy's mind worked like lightning. There was an urgency in his tone, a determination not to be put off. Interesting. He must have something very important on his mind to come all that way to see her.

A smile curved the softness of her lips. In the woman she was today, he'd never recognise the depressed-looking waif he'd briefly glared at in the November rain. Besides, she'd been wearing a cap, and an enveloping raincoat. The opportunity was too good to miss, and Roxy had no compunction in indulging in a little subterfuge with a man like him.

'Ann, I'll deal with this,' she said to the worried assistant. Ethan was creating something of a disturbance, and she ought to get him out of the shop.

'Oh, thanks, Rox——'

'Frocks!' she cried brightly, waving her carrier bags dangerously in the air, hoping Ethan hadn't heard her name properly. He did seem to be frowning oddly at her. 'Two fabulous Saint Laurent ones—raspberry and saffron silk—and a ravishing Lagerfeld in black velvet. Sensational, but I've spent a fortune!'

Roxy's grin encompassed Ethan. She was aware that her assistant laughed, stole a lingering look at Ethan and reluctantly resumed work. Roxy saw his tense face slightly relax as his fathoms-deep sea-green eyes took in Roxy's bright impact. Recognition at last, she thought triumphantly.

Her red hat had been tipped to the back of her head to show her dark, unruly hair and dancing, amused blue eyes. She was planning something and relishing the prospect of putting that plan into operation, but Ethan didn't know it, and, like all arrogant men of his kind, no doubt he imagined her elation was something to do with him.

With deliberate provocation, she sashayed towards him and leant elegantly against a counter, letting her gaze travel insolently up and down Ethan's hard and arrogantly masculine body.

He was quite a challenge, she thought, as his mocking eyes met hers cynically. Careful, came a warning voice. You adore challenges.

'You make a very effective entrance,' murmured Ethan, in tones the colour of honey. 'Bright and dazzling, like an exotic butterfly.'

There was just a tinge of huskiness beneath the smooth words to suggest a sensuality lurking beneath the powerful body. Immediately Roxy recognised him as a man on the prowl. He'd brow-beaten her assistant, but changed his tune for her. She didn't like that. Time someone taught him a lesson. It would be Roxy's pleasure.

'I do so dislike drabness, don't you?' she said sweetly, pointedly not looking at his boring, conventional suit. In addition, she steadfastly refused to admit that its elegance did more for him and his sex appeal than it decently should. 'Grey days are bad enough, without dressing so one's clothes merge into the murky background.'

His amused eyes scanned her outfit, lingering far too long on the curves of her breasts and hips.

'Some of us like to flaunt, some only like to reveal themselves to the chosen few,' he murmured.

Roxy bristled at the rebuke, but wouldn't let him know he'd affected her.

'Some of us are dull, some exciting,' she conceded.

'And which of those two categories fits me?' he murmured huskily.

Suddenly, she wasn't sure. There was a wickedness about him that wasn't obvious, but that seemed to be making her interested. That wouldn't do at all.

'At the moment, you're excited,' she purred. 'I heard you ... well, yelling at my assistant——'

'Your assistant?' he queried, his eyebrow rising fractionally.

'Mine. I own the chain of "Zest!" shops.'

'I see. Take your own products, do you?' he mocked. 'You look full of health pills.'

'I'm a good advertisement, aren't I?' she said jauntily, maintaining her fight for supremacy. 'Now, what made you lose your temper?' she asked in a patronising tone. 'Is something wrong?'

His eyes had become narrowed and hard at her thinly veiled criticism.

'I'm looking for Roxanne Page. I had this address from a solicitor. I'm beginning to wonder if she's not keen to meet me.'

'Well! That can't possibly be true,' exclaimed Roxy. 'Any girl would be thrilled.' He frowned at her from under his brows, and she realised she'd probably gone too far again, so carried on hastily, 'She can't be back, then. I'm afraid some girls don't know when lunchtime ends, do they? I'll show you where you can wait. Would you come with me, Mr...'

'Tremaine. It's Cornish,' he offered, holding out his big, capable-looking hand.

Very nice, thought Roxy. He uses his eyes a lot. No wonder women queue up for him. His steady gaze held hers for a few long seconds and, for that time, Roxy felt a faint panic at the dryness of her throat.

It was almost as if her fast-moving brain and body had been slowed down by huge brakes as his compelling eyes stilled her. An inner calm settled deep inside her, and she struggled against its lure. Peace was the enemy of drive and initiative. Her mind began to rev up again. He'd said something about being Cornish. She smiled to herself.

'Cornish? How quaint,' she murmured condescendingly. 'Isn't that the land of little pixies and meat pasties?'

To her delight, Ethan choked at the way she dismissed his ancient heritage in a few patronising words, and she gave him one of her dazzling smiles to compensate, letting her thick lashes flutter slightly. She'd keep him dangling until she knew why he'd come.

'We'll go upstairs, shall we, Mr Tremaine? I have offices there. You can tell me about Miss Page in comfort.'

'I like the sound of that,' he husked.

Roxy frowned. His eyes still mocked her. Now, why was that? Disconcertingly, he walked so close to her that their bodies rubbed, thigh to thigh, as they mounted the stairs. Her satin underwear slid seductively beneath her dress under the pressure, and she felt a little breathless from the sensation. He moved closer, to enjoy the feel of their bodies, and she was crowded against the banister.

Roxy nervously became aware of the contrasting softness of his well-cut suit, and the one-hundred-percent hard, muscled man which lay beneath it. It wasn't like her to allow men so much freedom to touch her on a slight acquaintance. But, she reasoned, she had to keep Ethan sweet, and put him off guard.

He let his hand drift across her back, under the pretence of reaching for the rail. Her spine tingled slightly. He was definitely making a play for her. The aristocratic Ethan Tremaine had been trapped in a web, spun by a servant's daughter. The idea amused Roxy.

'Your Miss Page,' he said in his deep voice. 'Will she be back soon, do you think?'

'Today you're in luck,' she said innocently, noting his eyes upon her. 'Roxanne has been known not to return for the afternoon at all, but I know for a fact that she won't play that trick today.'

'Do you, indeed? What an irritation she must be to you,' he said smoothly. 'And to all of us.'

'Oh? Why?' asked Roxy.

He shrugged. 'I've heard some dreadful things about her. Haven't you?' he asked with an innocent look.

'No, I haven't. Like...what?' she asked, worried. The only way he could have heard anything was from her letters to her mother, and they were pretty innocent.

He pursed his lips. 'I couldn't repeat gossip,' he said smugly.

Roxy could have hit him. She burned to know. She'd pretend she was on his side—he might confide in her. Pausing on the stairs, she touched his arm confidentially.

'You can't blame her. The girl has no breeding,' she said in an undertone.

His brows dropped in a slight frown; then, as Roxy patted his arm as if they both shared a distaste for such girls, her perfume delicately clouded the air between them. She felt his interest quicken, and the intensity of his green eyes warmed her brain and body in a disconcerting way.

'You didn't give me your name,' he murmured.

She pushed her lips into a thoughtful pout and darted a flirtatious look at his steady and quietly assessing eyes. Beside Ethan, she felt frivolous. He seemed so controlled and serious. These were qualities she'd never envied before. Usually she felt sorry for people who didn't laugh a lot, and enjoy life to the full. Suddenly she longed to be calm and deep, instead of dashing around in a swift and sometimes exhausted mad rush.

'My name?' she smiled brightly, stalling for time.

His mouth slowly curved into a smile. And she found, to her surprise, that the simple rearrangement of his features created an instant warmth down the central core of her body. Men didn't usually stir her so easily. Not with a mere smile! But, she mused, Ethan didn't look the kind who smiled often. She felt somehow privileged to be on the receiving end of one. It seemed a man didn't have to be full of dazzling grins and obvious admiration to charm birds off trees and women into bed.

This was ridiculous. His wretched smile had succeeded in turning her brain to treacle! Shaking her head in an irritated gesture, she recovered her composure. She didn't like the way she'd been effortlessly drawn by his magnetism. There was no need for her to go weak at the knees merely because a man smiled.

'Your name,' he coaxed.

Her wicked sense of humour pushed her on. 'Oh, dear. It seems so formal...' she demurred. 'Call me...' Her long black lashes fluttered coyly. 'Bubbles,' she said breathlessly.

A muscle twitched in his jaw and she wondered if she'd overdone it again. Bubbles! Controlling her laughter with difficulty, Roxy hurried up the stairs slightly ahead of Ethan, appropriately bubbling over with energy and excitement. Unfortunately, she'd forgotten her tendency to sway her hips in an exaggerated fashion when she was wearing her impossibly high heels. It must have been too much for him.

A firm hand caught her wrist and she was spun around so fast that she didn't have time to resist when he jerked her into his body.

'Bubbles, you say?' he asked. At her wide-eyed nod, he lifted one eyebrow cynically. 'How you do provoke a man. Quite beyond all belief. Well, I accept your challenge. We'll lock swords. To be honest, you've asked for it.'

To Roxy's astonishment, his head bent and he kissed her hard. If she hadn't liked it, she wouldn't have minded. Kisses weren't much, not usually. This was, and it became even more enjoyable when it suddenly lost its fierce assault and grew gentle. From the split second she saw the warning light in the ocean of his eyes, her body had begun to melt towards him, surrendering unconsciously before her brain had time to know of her own betrayal.

Tenderly his mouth roamed, moving with the kind of expertise Roxy appreciated, having suffered many ham-fisted assaults. This was carried out with such finesse that she was having difficulty breathing, and in her already over-excited state she was dangerously close to wanting the embrace to go further as she sank deeper into his arms.

'Very nice,' he murmured. 'What a surprise.'

'Don't——'

Her protest was stifled by his laughing mouth. How was she going to handle the situation now? Oh, lord! Ethan's lips were indescribably sweet, and his hands knew exactly what to do with her spine to give her pleasure. Someone save her!

'You seductive little wanton,' he muttered.

'I know,' she said heavily, expecting him to laugh and release her. She became alarmed; he grunted deeper in his throat and slid one hand to her neat rear.

'Show me how wanton you can be,' he urged.

Roxy wondered briefly how she could get out of this situation and win. The rhythm of his palm was becoming too pleasant. Gently his parted lips touched hers, coaxing. Roxy dearly wanted to pull away, yet her body nestled in closer to his, responding shockingly. Her lips were, astoundingly, returning his kisses, and with a sigh of helplessness she let her hands drift up to his neck and move lightly over the warm nape.

Ethan gave a satisfied growl and moved against her so that she could feel the hard angle of each hip—and the heat and hardness that rose between. Slowly her hands began to obey her and, still a little bemused, she pushed firmly against his chest. He moved back, with a perplexed look on his face. She suppressed the small fierce stabs from her defiant and treacherous nerve-endings, and summoned up a reproving lift of an eyebrow.

'I know.' He gave Roxy a slow, rueful grin, riveting her with his even white teeth. 'A bit sudden, wasn't it? Surprised me, too. You have yourself to blame,' he said thickly. 'A mere kiss isn't supposed to stir up so much . . . excitement,' he growled.

'Did it?' she asked casually, trying to make her lips move normally. What had happened to them?

'You know it did,' he declared, staring at her breasts. To her dismay they hardened beneath his eyes. Roxy blinked, stunned that he had that kind of effect on her.

Then her numbed brain began to operate her mouth again.

'I hope you're not intending to assault Miss Page in this way,' she said sharply.

He grinned. 'If she's like you, I might.'

'You . . . haven't seen her, then?' she asked in a rather unnaturally high voice.

Still amused, he seemed to be enjoying a private joke, and it irritated her. 'Briefly. She looked as if she was auditioning for the part of a tramp.'

Roxy flushed. She hadn't looked that bad. 'I think you ought to give me your message for her and go,' she said with a cool smile.

'Not angry, are you?' he asked engagingly. 'I had to pin you down for a moment, in case you flew away out of my sight. You were so elated and . . . well, so bubbling with life. Your nickname suits you. You seem to be spilling over with joy. No man could have resisted you. I saw no reason to bother.'

She was trapped, in more ways than one. In the role she'd adopted she had to pretend that casual kissing didn't mean much. She still hadn't extracted any information. Waving an airy hand of dismissal, Roxy gracefully acknowledged the likely truth of his remark, inexplicably feeling on top of the world. She should have been angry, but instead she simmered and seethed with suppressed energy, ignited by his kiss. Yet she remained wary. Judging by that recent experience, Ethan was a dangerous man. He took what he wanted, wherever he could find it. At the moment, he wanted her.

She knew how to handle him, though. He'd caught her off guard. Her surprising arousal made things more difficult, but not impossible. Patting his chest as if he were a naughty boy, she escaped from his clasp and moved towards the suite of offices, with Ethan following close behind. The hairs on the back of her neck lifted at the warmth of his breath there. It was irregular, like hers, and that knowledge added fuel to her inner fire.

Roxy preferred not to be shaken into awareness of her own physical self. It was a nuisance. She'd only wanted to string him along, and now she was struggling against being hooked too. If she'd had any sense she would never have flirted with him. She ought to have known from his reputation that he didn't need any encouragement.

It had given her quite a kick, though, to think that he had been shaken by the kiss. But perhaps this was how he fooled all the women, by letting them think they could crack his detachment, and melt his icy heart.

'You should be careful,' he said softly, 'throwing out signals in all directions.'

'Not signals,' she defended. 'I plead the excuse of elation. And champagne. My blood-vessels are full of it. I had a marvellous lunch at the Savoy,' she said casually, deciding to ignore what had happened, as if it meant nothing to her. 'I discussed plans to expand my business.'

'You're telling me that what happened between us was caused by alcohol and... *business*?' he asked, startled and affronted. 'Business is exciting to you?'

Roxy tried not to giggle. 'Oh, yes, Mr Tremaine,' she said, deliberately emphasising his name as they entered the offices. Joe's eyes opened wide in surprise. 'Exhilarating. It's the most exciting thing in the world to me.'

'That doesn't say much for your lovers, does it?' he murmured.

'Who needs men, when success can be so thrilling?' she said provocatively, knowing he'd hate the male sex to be relegated so casually and completely to second place in a woman's life.

Ethan looked appalled. His hand strayed beneath her jacket to spread around her tiny waist, and she dimpled coyly, gritting her teeth against the moulding of his palm over her buttocks.

'Whatever have the men around here been doing? I'm afraid they've given the male sex a bad name,' he said seductively. 'It looks as if you need someone to put you right. I think I'd better introduce you to a few experiences you won't forget in a hurry.'

Strangely, Roxy thought there had been a note of steel in his voice, but she was diverted when Joe coughed and shuffled papers innocently. She grinned, not taking Ethan's words seriously. He was merely thumping his chest, gorilla-style. It was the kind of macho response she would have expected from him.

In a quick, darting movement, she slid from Ethan's slow and insidiously creeping fingers, which had already reached her hip, and threw her hat on to the sofa, shaking her head as usual to release her hair. Then she slid off her jacket as if she were in a Soho strip club, and was rewarded by Ethan's heavy release of breath.

'Joe,' she said, feeling she held all the cards again, 'Mr Tremaine is here to speak to a member of the staff here. That flighty girl Roxanne Page.' Her eyes fixed him sternly, but thankfully Joe was far too used to her ways to show surprise.

'Oh, yes,' he said. 'The bossy one.'

Roxy's mouth twitched, the light in her eyes telling Joe that she'd deal with him later.

'Shall I . . . er . . . page Miss Page now?' asked Joe, deliberately putting Roxy on the spot.

'No,' said Ethan, his voice a little sharp around the edges. 'Don't do that yet.'

Secretly, Roxy felt that deep down he was angry about something. Ethan moved towards her like a wary animal, his body hard and tense as if he'd been alerted by a potential danger. He smiled, but the smile didn't wipe away the calculating look in his eyes. She shivered.

'There's no rush,' he continued, not taking his eyes off her for a second. 'Bubbles and I——'

He was halted mid-way as the hapless Joe covered up his explosion of laughter by pretending to drop a whole sheaf of papers.

'Oh, lord, aren't staff impossible nowadays?' sighed Roxy.

Hastily ushering Ethan into her office, she pushed him into a chair, ignoring his quick intake of breath at the décor. It must look a bit dazzling to people who weren't used to loads of sunshine colours together, she realised.

'Men can be so clumsy, can't they?' she beamed.

Ethan dragged his eyes from an orange sofa with scarlet and fuchsia cushions. Somehow, Roxy was aware that his sardonic glance had nothing to do with her unconventional colour scheme.

'I think your assistant was a little surprised to learn of your nickname,' he said slowly.

She flushed. To hide the tell-tale pinkening of her skin, she bent to dump her shopping on a spare chair.

'He's my secretary,' she corrected, avoiding the issue.

'You have a male secretary?' he queried.

'Of course,' she tossed. 'Doesn't every woman?'

This time there was a twist to the corner of his mouth. She knew instinctively that he didn't like the way she was putting down the male sex and pushing them into an inferior position. Normally Roxy wouldn't. She'd taken on Joe because he was the best of the interviewees. But Ethan riled her so much that he made her overplay her hand.

'Depends how she wants to spend her coffee breaks, I suppose,' he said insultingly.

Typical, she fumed inside, giving him a cool glance. This man wouldn't recognise female independence if

it hit him on the head. Pity he didn't know she was
sending him up.

Instead of going to her seat behind her desk, she
sat opposite Ethan to tease him better, and innocently
crossed her smooth legs. Her action rebounded on her,
as his gaze crawled hungrily up their slender length
and down again, resting with fascination on her highly
arched feet in the dainty shoes. Roxy felt as if he'd
trailed his hands lightly and sensually over her skin,
she was quivering so much. Without intending it to,
her tongue touched the corner of her poppy-coloured
mouth and he leaned back languidly in his chair, his
eyes mesmerising her.

'Are you going to give me a personal fashion show?'
he asked in a slow drawl.

It was unbelievable how jittery she felt. He didn't
know her, and yet he was propositioning her. And the
odd thing was, she felt flattered. Ethan wouldn't normally waste time in chatting up women. His first kiss
had been so devastating that he probably moved
smoothly to total seduction in one fluid movement,
she thought wryly.

'How unusual for a man to have an interest in
clothes,' she said sweetly.

The green eyes half closed and his mouth became
sultry. 'I haven't,' he said huskily. 'Only the female
body.'

Beneath the banter was a serious message of intent.
Roxy felt her hands stupidly fly to protect her breasts.
In panic, she turned it into a comic gesture.

Confused, she was finding it difficult to separate
what she wanted consciously from the needs of her
subconscious. Of course, she had to soften Ethan up,
so that he gave out information.

Her chaotic feelings shocked her. Contrary to her
own arrogant beliefs, she'd been as much of an easy

pushover as all the other women he'd fondled! That was really galling. Though she couldn't tell him what she really felt about his insolent seduction. Not yet. It would be sweet revenge when she did.

'You won't get me out of my clothes that easily,' she said tartly.

How amusing, when he discovered who she was! He wouldn't be so quick to flirt, knowing she was a housekeeper's daughter.

'I must try a little harder, then, mustn't I?' he husked. 'How about dinner first?'

'Dinner first?' she repeated, opening her blue eyes wide. 'So you're a patient man?' she taunted, suggesting that only a slowcoach would wait that long for her.

His jaw clenched and a battle light glinted in his eyes. Evidently he wasn't, thought Roxy in alarm.

'You,' he muttered, looking daggers at her, 'are asking for trouble. And I'm going to see you get it.'

Hastily she retreated behind her desk and flicked down the intercom switch. There was a hard and unyielding quality about him beneath that strong, still façade, and she had an idea that his determined streak matched hers—and perhaps outstripped it. This could be the moment to probe into his intentions and then get on with her day.

'Joe, see if Miss Page is in Despatch, would you?' she asked hastily.

'If you think it's worth the effort,' he muttered.

'I'm in no hurry to bring anyone else into this room,' said Ethan, treating her to a long, meaningful look that somehow also held menace. 'I'd much rather stay up here in your ivory tower, watching you breathe.'

His eyes fastened on her breasts, and Roxy became conscious of the fact that her breathing was quite disconcertingly shallow and was causing her ribcage to rise alarmingly.

Joe saved her. 'There's no Miss Page in Despatch,' he said abruptly.

'Try everywhere else,' she said, clearing her throat to rid herself of whatever was making her speak croakily.

'Now,' she continued, turning to Ethan, with a slightly wavering smile, 'perhaps you'd tell me what this is all about. Why are you here to see Roxanne? A boyfriend, are you?'

He gave an involuntary shudder which made Roxy's spine go rigid with fury. A derisive sneer drew down his mouth.

'Good lord, no! Give me a little credit for good taste. She's not my type at all. No, it's a business matter. But why talk about her?'

'What kind of business matter?' she asked sweetly. 'You see, if it's important, then we must do our utmost to find her. She's proving to be awfully elusive, isn't she?'

'Oh, I wouldn't say that. I could see her tomorrow anyway. I've finished all my other business in London. I'm staying in London tonight. I very much want you to have dinner with me. Will you?'

Roxy was intrigued. What ever could the high and mighty Tremaine want with lowly little Miss Page?

'I usually work late,' she demurred.

'So we eat late,' he shrugged. 'You're worth waiting for. The evening may prove to be more interesting than you could imagine,' he continued, leaning forwards. 'I find your situation intriguing.'

'You mean...my success? The fact that my business skill has enabled me to control several stores?' She gave a feline smile. 'And women.' The smile broadened. 'And men.'

He shot her a suspicious look, but she kept her face bland, even when she met his stone-cold eyes.

'I wondered about your...er...skills.' Slowly, insolently, he raked her body as if considering her more carnal qualities. 'A clever woman could get far with a body like yours.'

'Only if men were silly enough to fall for that kind of manipulation,' she countered.

His grin flashed, sudden and startling. 'Some might. I wouldn't.'

'Oh, don't you think so?' She smiled.

His steady regard unnerved her. He couldn't know, could he? Roxy racked her brain. She hadn't said or done anything that could have made him connect her with the woman he'd seen three months ago.

'You're finding this an interesting situation, aren't you?' he observed. 'Me, looking for Roxanne and finding you. I look forward to knowing you better. You would be a worthy adversary for any man, I think,' he said thoughtfully.

She was about to ask him what he meant when Joe buzzed.

'Sorry to butt in. I've searched everywhere except your office and Miss Page isn't to be found. Er...there's a slight problem out here. Could you come out a moment?'

Roxy smiled apologetically at Ethan and made a sultry exit, relief flooding her face when she shut her office door behind her.

'What the heck are you playing at?' seethed Joe. 'How long do we play this game?'

'Till I know why he's here,' whispered Roxy. 'Sorry, Joe, but I have a feeling he's up to something.'

'Yeah. You,' he muttered. 'He's got bedside lights glinting in his eyes. You watch what you're doing. You're a little bit interested in him, aren't you?'

'Rubbish,' she said, and answered the phone as it rang. 'Who? Penhaligon? I remember, the Cornish solicitor... No, I couldn't possibly! Why...? Good heavens! How dramatic! Is that really still done nowadays? Excuse me a moment.'

Roxy covered the mouthpiece, frowning, 'Joe, could I go down to Cornwall on Monday?'

He consulted her diary. 'Only if it's important enough to ditch your appointments with Jason Rees about the Bristol launch and Ophelia about redecorating your flat. Apart from——'

'OK. Thanks. Yes, I'll be there,' she told the solicitor. 'Ten o'clock. Goodbye.'

'What's all that about?' asked Joe, seeing her thoughtful face.

'They've unearthed a will,' she said slowly. 'One made by Mrs Tremaine. They want me to be present for the reading.'

'Oh, come on,' scoffed Joe. 'That's film stuff.'

'Not in Cornwall, it isn't,' she answered absently. 'Mr Penhaligon says the family still demands a proper reading. Now, why me? Do you think Mrs Tremaine has left me something? Mother said I brightened her life with my chatty letters and general news.' She chewed her inner lip, thinking. 'So that's why Ethan is here. I bet he's trying to do me out of my little bequest. Cheapskate!'

'What are you going to do?'

Roxy's eyes hardened to cold blue chips. 'Pump him for all he's worth,' she grated. 'Find out what his devious mind is planning and beat him at his own game. Tonight should be interesting.'

'Challenges, challenges. Watch it,' warned Joe anxiously.

'Joe,' she said, brimming over with the anticipation of a stimulating evening, 'I'll put my best frock on and use all my wiles. He's already eager.'

Perversely, she was a little disappointed that Ethan had fallen for her rather obvious approach.

'But supposing he has another attempt at transferring your lipstick to his mouth again?' asked Joe innocently.

Roxy flushed scarlet. 'That was...'

'Quick work on your part?' suggested Joe.

'An accident,' she said sharply.

'Mmm. The fatal sort.'

'I'll cope with him.'

Joe gave her an old-fashioned look and she sighed. 'OK,' she said. 'You're right. He's devastating. But I'm not going to invite him up to my flat. We'll have a cosy dinner with low lights and plenty of wine and he'll tell me all.'

Joe shrugged, evidently not believing her. Irritated, she eyed the closed door of her office, behind which Ethan lurked. A small spiral of excitement curled within her at the thought of entering. Joe was right, Ethan had given all the signs of confidence. He expected her to sleep with him that night, and looked perfectly capable of backing up that expectation with force if necessary. All the more reason to extract the information she wanted and get out early, before things went too far.

Sense before senses, mind over matter, she told herself. Yet humour wasn't helping this time. Roxy felt like a girl going on her first date, and that made her confused. It had been years since butterflies had flocked in her stomach, seeking escape.

She pushed her fingers through her hair in a feminine gesture and strolled to the door, conscious of her pallor and the trembling in her legs.

CHAPTER THREE

ROXY slid around the door, a charming smile pinned to her face. The smile faltered a little when she saw Ethan. He'd been pacing up and down, but stood stock still when she entered, his hands thrust in his pockets so that his dark jacket was pushed aside, giving her eyes unrestrained access to the strong lines of his body. Something in his pose made her think that he was challenging and warning her. Her lashes swept downwards, reluctantly admiring his powerful legs where the material of his trousers had been drawn tight over the muscles.

Roxy knew his stance was deliberate, to emphasise the fact that he was a superior male and she a mere female. A little annoyed by his manner, Roxy started jauntily across the floor. But Ethan met her half-way, a calculating look in his eyes.

'I don't want to take up any more of your time now,' he said huskily, holding her arms lightly. 'I have a couple of things to check out. I'll book a table somewhere quiet, for eight. Tell me where I can pick you up.' His hands had begun to slide gently upwards in possession.

'Quiet?'

Roxy's lips parted to protest that she wanted somewhere noisy and full of people, but he drew her into his body. Through the fabric of her dress, he felt warm and solid—and unnervingly inescapable.

'Quiet,' he repeated in a tone threaded with steel. 'I don't have long in London, and I have every intention of discovering a great deal about you before

38

I leave. And,' he said, his eyes glittering like a green, sunlit sea, 'I intend to explore you. Every inch. Hour by hour.'

Roxy swallowed as her heart leapt into her throat. Getting involved with Ethan Tremaine was going to be suicidal. And she might even enjoy it, she groaned inwardly, as his warm, questing hands slid to her shoulders, pressing her harder against him.

Desperately she struggled to find something witty to say, to cool the situation. 'Explore? You sound like——'

'Stop hiding behind words,' he muttered, soothing her mounting alarm with gentle movements over her spine. 'You don't have to put on that sparkling rep-artee *all* the time.'

The pressure on her back increased till she could feel the pads of each deeply massaging finger. What was he doing to her? she thought incoherently. Roxy swayed, then let the whole of her body relax help-lessly. She couldn't tear her eyes away from his brooding face, which was coming closer and closer.

'Dinner?' he murmured, almost against her pouting lips.

Roxy's inner struggle showed. Ethan merely let one hand drift to the curve of her waist and gave her one of his gentle smiles. It would be all right, she told herself. They would be sitting at a table, opposite each other.

Nervous, and telling herself that she was a fool to take the risk, she nodded, her eyes wary. Reluctantly he released her and she immediately wanted to close the space between them. And resented that feeling.

'Eight is fine,' she said coolly. 'Ten, Wharf Reach.'

'Thank the lord I don't have long to wait,' he breathed, his hand reaching out.

Roxy watched in an agony of suspense as it rose and lightly caressed the soft hairs of her cheek, the action making her head tilt back a little and her eyes droop drowsily. A shudder ran through him. He seemed about to say something else—perhaps, she thought wildly, to ask if he might stay—but his hand fell, leaving Roxy with an intense feeling of disappointment.

'I'd better go,' he muttered, a tremor vibrating his voice.

She nodded, incapable of speech. Slowly Ethan walked to the door, where he turned, frowning, his dark-clad figure indistinct, to her hazy sight, against the black paintwork. Roxy was drawn to his remorseless eyes and saw in them a mirror of her own confusion and desire.

'I want you, you know that,' he breathed harshly. 'You feel the same. For pity's sake, we hardly know each other! Why?'

Flustered, she tried to pull away from the magnetic field that pulled them inexorably to one another. She didn't like losing control, ever.

'Mass outbreak in hormones, I suppose,' she croaked.

He glared. 'Don't try to escape me,' he said softly. 'I'm not allowing this to affect me forever. I don't like it. I'll get you out of my system soon. Divert me with humour if you wish; you'll still end up where I want you.' His eyes glowed with a primeval hunger. 'Beneath me. Naked and hungry,' he whispered starkly.

The ravening cruelty in his face shocked her. 'Hungry?' she jerked out. 'I thought you said we'd have dinner——'

With a frightening ignition of his entire body, and startling Roxy by the rough curse that erupted through his teeth, Ethan strode across the room in a violent movement and pinned her against the wall. His body crushed her relentlessly. Bending his head, just as Roxy's brain grew numb at the feel of his hard, aroused heat, he concentrated purely on kissing her until she could hardly breathe and her lips had bloomed and swollen beneath his ardour.

'Provocation again,' he muttered, letting his mouth sweep her jaw. 'Sweet provocation. You really must be more careful.'

'Brute,' she whispered, as a languorous, sensual weakness crept into every corner of her body. 'Let me go.'

'Try to sound a little more convincing,' he suggested, amused.

Roxy flushed and then flinched under the pleasurable slide of his questing fingers as they caressed the nape of her neck.

'I—I've changed my mind. I don't want to have dinner,' she said unevenly.

'Neither do I, but it's a ritual,' he drawled. 'Let's keep up the pretence, at least.'

His bluntness shocked her. 'No...'

His tongue touched her lips and she clamped them shut quickly. He smiled deep into her eyes and used his thumb to force her lips apart, then bent quickly to kiss her, the tip of his tongue hard and erotic on the inside of her mouth.

A beautiful pain, as fast and slicing as the blade of a knife, ripped through her body. Frantically Roxy tried to speak, but found she had given a little moan instead.

I won't let him win, she thought, summoning up her reserves of will-power.

'Ethan,' she muttered, shaking from the effort of refusing him. She usually had everything she wanted. 'I demand——'

'Demand all you like. I'm taking no notice.'

She quivered. His words had vibrated against her mouth erotically. The rhythm of his relentless fingers was clouding her conscious mind. He'd trapped her with her own secret longing for a man who could truly arouse her dormant sexuality. Now she'd found him and didn't know how to handle its implications.

'You're moving too fast——'

His fingers slowed. 'Is that more to your liking?' he whispered. 'Slow and seductive?' From the mocking smile he gave her, he'd known just what she'd meant.

'I won't be pushed along at your pace,' she scowled.

'You go at whatever pace you like,' he said lazily. The eyes narrowed. 'I'll continue to move at mine.'

She tightened her mouth. 'You can't ignore me——'

'Oh,' he growled, deep in his throat, 'I'm not ignoring you.'

Nor was he. Roxy whimpered as his hands travelled tantalisingly down to her thighs and he leaned hard into her. In his present state, Ethan was incapable of ignoring her, she thought frantically, and then was swamped by a rising tide of shame.

'Joe might come in,' she mumbled, hopelessly. Ethan didn't know how to play fair. Roxy jerked and moaned at the excruciatingly sharp stabs of desire as his fingers caught each hard peak of her full breasts. 'Don't,' she whispered, revelling in the sweet torture. Her head rolled. The pleasure continued mercilessly, and she began to make soft little sounds in her throat.

'I hope you're getting hungry,' he said thickly. 'I have one hell of an appetite.'

His hand curved beneath each breast for a brief moment, and then he'd gone.

Roxy reached out to the desk and clutched at it for support. She felt terrified by the fierce, frightening attraction. It had taken her by storm.

Her shaking hand reached for the intercom. 'No calls, Joe,' she said tremulously.

'You all right?' he asked.

'Suffering from after-effects,' she managed.

'Oh, hangover. Well, if you will celebrate your brilliance,' he said, unsympathetically.

Roxy sank into a deep armchair, kicked her shoes off and curled up, a complete contrast to the woman who had breezed into the office that morning. Her face was pale and serious, her eyes glazed as she wrestled with her inner conscience.

Yet, every time her mind came around to deciding what questions she was going to ask Ethan Tremaine about his intentions as far as Roxanne Page was concerned, she fell into a softly cloaked dream which followed an imaginative picture of his more sensual plans. Judging by the way he'd reduced her to a mass of quivering, melting urges, his lovemaking would be spectacularly torrid. Wretched man!

Roxy bit her lip. Her plan had backfired disastrously. But she wouldn't give up. She'd succeed, somehow. What she needed to do was to work like mad, leaving herself hardly any time to get ready. That way, she wouldn't dwell on what he might or might not do. And she *must* remember he only wanted a one-night stand, to fill his empty bed.

Her glare became ferocious. Deliberately she worked on developing a scouring resentment, to wipe away any faint desire. She wasn't going to end up the victim of Ethan's casual sexuality, not even if he tried all night to seduce her with that throaty voice and extraordinarily sensitive hands.

After dinner, she'd thank him and say goodnight. He'd be stunned to get such a poor reward for all his efforts! Roxy began to brighten up. Nothing would give her greater pleasure than to prove to him he wasn't as irresistible as he seemed to think.

She did work late that evening, far later than she'd intended. It was seven-thirty by the time the taxi dropped her at the entrance to the fashionable Docklands site. Still, that was long enough to shower and change. On the way back she'd been going through her wardrobe in her mind, trying to decide what to wear. She still hadn't come to a decision. Sexy or frosty? Sophisticated or bombshell?

As she made her way across the deserted courtyard, something about the steps behind made her glance over her shoulder. Two men were coming towards her. She crossed the yard and so did they. Then she crossed back again and was alarmed when they did, too, one of the men giving a nasty laugh. Her feet clattered on the iron staircase which led up to her elegant front door in the converted warehouse. The men came after her. Exclusive or not, the area attracted one or two dubious characters, and Roxy—terrified of the very idea of violence—had long been prepared.

Quickly she dipped her hand in her bag and brought out her shriek alarm, ready to set it off if she was threatened. The back of her neck prickled when she quickened her step and found that the men were gaining on her.

'Going home, darling?' one of them leered.

She turned, saw their menacing expressions and flicked the catch on the alarm.

'Yes, and so are you, I think,' she cried, flinging the canister at them. The emerging shrill scream panicked her as much as the men, and she ran full tilt up the steps, straight into a solid wall of flesh.

She yelled and beat at the unyielding chest, then found her arms pinioned behind her and her face pressed against the man's white shirt.

'All right! It's me! They've run off,' growled Ethan into her ear.

'Oh, thank goodness!' she gasped. Weak with relief, she sagged, grateful for his protective strength, and enjoying it too, as his hands warmed her waist.

By the sounds around her, neighbours in the other flats were emerging from their front doors, curious to see what the noise was about. At last, the awful synthetic scream faded and finally stopped altogether, leaving a blissful silence.

Roxy emerged, red-faced, from Ethan's chest. She always seemed to be trembling when he held her, she thought crossly.

'It's all right, it was only me,' she called in embarrassment to everyone. 'I'm sorry.'

'It would be you,' grinned her nearest neighbour, an airline pilot she'd once dated. 'Does that fellow with you know what he's letting himself in for?'

'Open your door,' said Ethan, scowling. 'I hate public displays.'

Without thinking, still disturbed by the lurking men, she produced her key, and it was only when they walked into her hall that she wondered why she'd calmly let him in, and what he was doing there so early.

'Feel OK?' asked Ethan.

'Of course,' she lied coolly.

'Good grief!' he exclaimed, diverting her thoughts. 'Can you actually live with that colour?'

He was staring at the eye-searing yellow drapes hanging from the ceiling. 'It's stimulating,' she said defensively, feeling that she might burst into tears if he criticised her at this moment. The incident had upset her more than she'd thought. She loathed being touched by people she disliked, and she was a physical coward.

'Is that what it is?' he said in wonder.

He wandered around the enormous room, fingering the gaudily dyed calico curtains which billowed in enormous, extravagant folds. The floor shone a glossy black, and the chrome furniture gleamed softly as Roxy lit candles everywhere, the flickering yellow light enhancing the cheerful sunny reds and oranges of the comfortable chairs. Everywhere was in a mess, as usual. She never found time to tidy up much, resorting to having a blitz every now and then.

'More decorative than domestic, aren't you?' he observed.

'I'm a business woman. Oh, lord. I've got to sit down a minute,' she muttered.

'So you're not as tough as you make out.'

He looked as if he might come and comfort her, given half a chance, and suddenly that was the last thing she wanted. As jittery as she was, she preferred to howl in solitude. Snuggling up to that big chest and throwing her arms around his neck would be too appealing. He'd take advantage, and where would she be then?

'Don't come near me. I'm on edge,' she said, in mounting agitation. 'I've had a long day, those men unnerved me—and the alarm unnerved me even more. How do they get such a lot of noise in such a small can? And to cap it all, you're early. I need space, I need a little peace and quiet to myself.'

'You'll have the whole evening,' he said quietly, 'if that's what you want. I'm afraid I can't keep our date. I came early to tell you I have to return home.'

Roxy felt a flash of disappointment. 'Oh, no bother. I've loads of things to do. It's OK.'

'Is it? You don't sound too sure. I'm sorry—I'd much rather be here with you than careering down motorways.'

His sincerity cheered Roxy. Then she remembered to her dismay that she didn't know why he'd been searching for her in the first place. It was important that she did. Ethan might be a swine, or he might be decent. One way or the other, she had to find out.

'What about Roxanne Page?' she asked abruptly. 'You were going to see her tomorrow.'

'I know.' He hesitated. 'How well do you know her? What kind of relationship is there between you?'

'As the owner of the shop, I sometimes have to remind her of her position,' said Roxy carefully. 'Tell her to be serious, that kind of thing. She takes it pretty well.'

'I'm sure she does,' he said, his mouth twisting wryly. 'Then perhaps you'd tell her I was trying to find her and will be writing later. I was in London, you see, and thought I'd drop in with my suggestion in person, rather than put it in a letter.'

'I could tell her what your business with her involves; perhaps sound her out for you,' suggested Roxy, probing desperately. 'Let me take a message, please.'

'Kind of you,' he murmured. He surveyed her for a long, thoughtful moment. 'Well, seeing as it's you . . . why not? Let her know that I want to arrange for her to have a small pension.'

'What for?' frowned Roxy, astounded. That didn't sound like heartless Ethan Tremaine.

'Her mother died in service to mine. It would be churlish not to recognise that,' he said quietly. 'She'll know what it's all about.'

A pension. He was offering her money for nothing. Roxy's face lit up. Generosity was more than she expected from him. Perhaps he'd been misjudged by those who'd criticised him in the past. People often got the wrong idea about others.

'I must go,' he muttered. 'My sister is anxious. She doesn't want to be alone tonight.'

Roxy's nods might have been vigorous, but her eyes were treacherously pleading for him not to leave just yet.

'Please!' he growled. 'Don't tempt me to stay! Are you still nervous about those men?'

'Yes. I am. They might come back and take their revenge for being half deafened,' she said shakily. 'That's what I'd do, you see, if someone had thrown a screaming alarm at me.'

'I don't like leaving you,' he muttered. 'Damnation! If only Annabel...' He scowled, checking himself. 'My sister is upset,' he said tightly.

Was that anything to do with finding the will? she wondered. But her mind was drawn back to Ethan, and the diminishing gap between them. A bridge was being built by both of them, it seemed, one made from a flowing electrical charge that was linked to every one of her nerve-endings and terminated in her brain.

'Ethan...'

Her hands fluttered as they moved slightly to call him to her, and she quickly clenched them. But he'd seen, and interpreted the movement correctly.

To her utter joy he began to walk towards her as if he was in a dream, his gaze never once leaving her face. She closed her eyes, unable to bear the intensity that burned in the dark pupils. She heard his footsteps on the painted boards, then knew by the shivering sensation all over her skin that he was standing beside her.

'You need a holiday,' he said softly. 'Why don't you come with me tonight, to Cornwall? It would be a mad thing to do, on the spur of the moment, but I can't go without asking you. I'd be a fool not to.'

'A holiday?' she repeated, longing to cry 'yes'.

'Why not?' His hands dropped to her shoulders and began a slow massage that had Roxy gritting her teeth in an effort not to respond by groaning with pleasure. 'I live in a beautiful part of the world. It's very restful.' The insistent movement of his fingers was inexorably heating her body and melting her bones. Roxy felt that she was being manipulated in more ways than one. 'It's Saturday tomorrow. Can't you take time off? What fun is it being the boss if you can't play hookey sometimes?' he asked, in a soft growl.

It was so tempting. She had to go down to Carnock in a couple of days anyway. What could be better than to travel with him? On the way, she could tell him who she was, and explain at leisure. They could exchange information and get to know one another. Suddenly Roxy badly wanted to know why there was such a contradiction between her mother's report on Ethan's reputation and the very desirable man here in her flat.

Or was he merely putting over a slick charm that was fooling her?

'I didn't think you were the kind of girl who took long to make decisions,' he said softly. His mouth pressed against the nape of her neck and a shudder ran through her as his lips warmly explored, running lightly over her sensitised skin. 'Do you really want to spend tonight here alone, waiting and listening for any suspicious sound outside?' he coaxed. 'Come home with me.' His mouth was sweeping tiny kisses along the line of her jaw, and Roxy gripped the arms of her chair to prevent herself from crying out.

'Your sister,' she croaked, thinking of the haughty Annabel. Although, she thought wryly, his sister might give Roxy a different reception if she turned up in a Dior leisure suit and trailing clouds of expensive perfume.

'No problem. Don't give her another thought. Please come. I have to go, but I don't want to lose you. I'm determined not to leave you here. Why should I let other men climb the magic staircase?' he asked huskily.

'Iron. It's iron,' she said, twisting her head around to look at him with laughing eyes.

'You're doing it again,' he chided gently. 'Every time I get serious, you lighten the atmosphere. So I'll just have to make it heavy again, won't I?'

His hand slid to cradle her breast, lifting it slightly, and Roxy's eyes opened in shock. Then, before she could stop him, he had eased his big frame to balance on the arm of the chair and was kissing her, his lips firm and demanding. Her lethargy vanished as his mouth crushed her doubts into oblivion.

'I'll help you pack,' he muttered thickly. 'We could have one hell of a weekend. Oh, you taste good! We have a great deal of pleasure awaiting us, Bubbles. I guarantee you'll be a different woman afterwards.'

Yes, she thought, Bubbles would have miraculously turned into Roxanne Page! Ethan was very persistent. It wouldn't be a bad idea to establish the ground rules.

'It might be inconvenient. Unless you have a spare bed already made up,' she said hesitantly.

His eyes searched hers, amused. 'I was thinking we might share mine,' he said in a velvet voice, infinitely seductive.

'Don't rush me,' she whispered.

'Rush you! It's not my doing, this tempest that's hit us both.' Ethan turned over her palm and began to follow the intricate lines there. 'I didn't want to be hit over the head and knocked sideways by a sophisticated townie,' he said, his smile taking the sting out of his words. 'But, since I have, I'm enjoying the way the wind is blowing me.'

'Is that how you see me? A townie?' she asked. That would normally have pleased her, to be thought of as chic and groomed for city life. Yet because he was a countryman she wanted him to see her barefoot and casual, with her face scrubbed. Maybe he wouldn't be so attracted, she thought ruefully. Men were so contrary.

'Yes,' he sighed regretfully. 'I can't see you liking the country much. I could take you to Plymouth shopping, of course...'

'I'll come,' she said, suddenly coming to a decision. 'I can fit in anywhere. I'm tremendously adaptable, you'll see.'

Ethan's eyes crinkled at the corners and his slashing grin threw her brain into reverse.

'You'll come? Now?'

'I'll pack as fast as I can,' she promised. 'On the condition that we sleep in separate beds tonight—and every other night I stay. I don't want the disapproval of your sister. Nor do I want a cheap affair.'

'It would never be that,' he said quietly. For a heartbeat, the world stilled.

Roxy knew something incredible was happening to her and she was content. Despite this crazy, mad decision, the sensation she had was one of peace and serenity.

She'd put on a geranium-pink leisure suit in a soft, flattering velour which clung where it touched the lush fullness of her breasts and hips, leaving little to the imagination. Roxy was happy with her body and wanted to be alluring for Ethan. This was the beginning of something special. Into her dark hair she twisted a long coral-coloured scarf which exactly matched her nail polish and lipstick.

She knew that her eyes were diamond-bright with anticipation and excitement. Business success had nothing on this! It was extraordinary how easily and completely he'd vanquished her resentment and suspicions. The feelings she had left were so good and so powerful that Roxy was content to drift along with them, letting them take her where they might.

It had taken a very special man to arouse her physically almost to distraction: that man was special enough to have carved a niche for himself in her emotions, too. At the moment it was a small seed of contentment and harmony, but she knew intuitively that it would grow and change their lives. She knew.

'Shall we leave before my curtains curl up miserably at the competition?' she teased happily, emerging from her bedroom.

Ethan stopped his scowling pace and took in her sparkling eyes and laughing mouth.

'I think we'd better leave before I teach you a very interesting lesson,' he said, unsmiling.

'Here's my overnight bag,' she breathed, wide-eyed at his intensity.

She followed him down the staircase, devouring every line of his body, longing to reach out and feel the width of his hard-set shoulders. When they reached the courtyard, his arm reached for her waist and she slipped to his side, revelling in their closeness. Enjoying the touch of one another, they walked to his car in silence.

Black and glossy, she observed, with approval. Very fast, beautiful lines. Like him. Irresistible. Her hand slid over the curve of the bonnet.

'You like touching things, don't you?' he said, watching.

'I always have,' she admitted, slipping gracefully into the passenger seat, stretching her long legs out.

'I thought so. Odd that you should choose such an unsociable occupation.'

The engine roared into life and they moved off. She felt as if she'd run away and was suddenly free from all responsibilities. It was a heady sensation.

'I wasn't always rich, independent and successful,' she pointed out with a smile. 'My mother rather pushed me into nursing, but I was hopeless.'

'Because?' he asked.

'I spent too long chatting to the patients. They were so interesting,' she said, smiling at the memory. 'I was a dab hand at persuading people to take their treatment and enjoy their stay, but I hated the boring routine. Sister and I fell out a bit too often.'

'Still, it's a long haul from nursing to running a health store.'

She nodded. 'When I left the hospital, I reacted with my usual immoderation and left England altogether. I became a dental assistant in the States.'

'What brought you back?' he probed.

'Homesickness and the realisation that I'm not cut out to serve other people. I prefer to call the tune,' she said, sighing at her flawed character. 'I worked terribly hard to build up my business.'

'Are you ruthless? Selfish?'

'When I want something. Are you?' she asked suddenly.

'Very,' he answered crisply. 'More than I dare allow anyone to know.'

She shivered a little. Would he be very angry to find out her deception? Maybe this wasn't the time to tell him. She bit her lip.

'I have a problem, you see.' His face was dark and shuttered, the profile harsh. 'It may interfere with our weekend.'

'Maybe I shouldn't have come unannounced——'

'No. Your appearance won't surprise anyone. I might be worrying unnecessarily, but...' The granite jaw tightened.

'Tell me,' she urged. 'I'd be interested.'

'My mother died in December,' he explained. Roxy frowned. She should have told him who she was by now. 'I inherited the family home. Now my sister thinks that there's a possibility some of the land may not belong to me.'

'Is there much land?' she asked curiously.

His hands clenched the wheel and the car surged into the fast lane. For a few moments he appeared to be concentrating on the road ahead.

'Quite large for a Cornish farm. My land, of about a hundred and fifty acres, adjoined Carnock, my mother's estate, which is roughly the same size. With her death, there's now three hundred acres.'

Roxy gasped. 'You can't mind losing a bit of that!' she cried, trying to visualise what three hundred acres looked like. He must spend all day looking after fields or cows, or whatever he did on the farm. It struck her as odd that she didn't know what kind of farming he was involved in.

'You don't understand,' he said, his eyes resting thoughtfully on her. 'I've only just won that land back. I have no intention of letting any of it go again. You see, my parents divorced when I was ten,' he said. 'The huge original Carnock estate was split in two. My mother stayed in Carnock House, while father went to live on the adjoining land in a caravan till a new home could be built. I went with my father.'

'Why?' she asked quietly, seeing how cold and distant he'd suddenly become. The story must hurt him to tell. Roxy was certain that there was a good reason for his alleged indifference to his ailing mother.

'How do you choose in those circumstances?' He drew in a deep breath. 'In the end, it comes down to whom you love best, and maybe who has shown you most love. That was easily my father. But I'd reckoned without the agony of wrenching myself away from my beloved home. It's so beautiful. Without seeing it, no one could imagine what the sheer harmony of nature can do to your soul.'

'Didn't you visit your mother and...' Her voice trailed away. She'd known the answer, but hadn't reckoned on his reaction.

'Visit her?' he bit out viciously. 'Most days I wished her in hell!'

'You can't mean that about your own mother——'

'Disappointed by my heartlessness?' he snapped. 'You don't know what she was like. I'll just say that she made my father's life a misery and finally destroyed him. Then her warped mind tried to ruin mine, too. Every day of my life, till I inherited Carnock again, I ached to walk its land. Imagine a ten-year-old boy miserably walking along the fence that barred him from the places he'd played. Imagine,' he said his voice dropping to a bare whisper, 'a thirty-year-old man, still aching, still burning at the cruelty of Fate.'

'I can understand you'd be resentful——'

'More than that,' he growled deeply. 'I seethed with anger at the way Carnock was declining. Every day I'd torture myself, year in, year out, staring longingly at the fields, the barns and the gardens as they became unworked, derelict, unkempt. Unloved.'

'You had a new home. I'd have made the best of things and——'

'*You* might. Unless you experience it personally, you can't know what it's like to be part of a family that has lived in one place for centuries. There's a sense of belonging that far outweighs any rational thought. I hated my mother for casting me out. I felt like Cain, thrown out of Paradise. That's how I saw Carnock: as God's little acre. You'll understand when you arrive; even a hard-bitten city lover like you would appreciate its extraordinary beauty.'

'I'm sure no one's going to take it from you,' she said, hurt by his assessment of her. She might not know much about the country, but she always enjoyed looking at it on the television and on car journeys. If Carnock was as lovely as he claimed, then she'd like it too.

'Really?' he drawled.

Roxy's head turned slowly. 'Why should they?' she asked, warily. Did he know something she didn't? She prayed that the will didn't come between them. A premonition was telling her that it might. 'How . . . how could they?'

'How, indeed?' he muttered, his jaw clenching. 'I've spent too long yearning to be at Carnock to be denied now.' He shot her a glance and she quailed at the cold glitter of his ice-green eyes. 'I don't mind telling you, I think I'd kill anyone who tried to take it from me,' he added with soft savagery.

CHAPTER FOUR

Roxy shivered at the intense passion in his voice. She couldn't understand someone feeling that strongly about bricks and mortar, let alone about fields and trees. Home was the place you went back to when you finished work. For her, it had once been other people's homes. When her father had died of cancer soon after Roxy was born, her mother had gratefully gone to live and work in a big London house nearby, taking Roxy with her.

Later, just before her mother changed jobs and moved to Carnock, Roxy had lived in the nurses' home and shared an apartment in New York. She'd only just acquired her own flat, but she wasn't emotionally attached to it. Ethan's passion was impossible for her to understand.

The situation had gone far enough. She must come clean.

'Ethan, there's something I must tell you,' she said, hesitantly. 'I—I—oh, this is awful! I've sort of deceived you.'

His mouth tightened into a hard line. 'Have you?' he asked, as if unsurprised. His tone wasn't very encouraging.

This was more difficult than she thought. 'I've been rather stupid,' she admitted. 'You'll need to listen to all of my explanation if it's to make any sense.'

'All right, then,' he said harshly. 'Let's hear it.'

Roxy dearly wanted him to think well of her again, and almost backed out. But he'd only mistrust her if she did—after all, there was the reading of the will on Monday, and she'd have to announce who she was then.

'When you turned up asking for Roxanne Page, I was suspicious,' she began, her fingers locked tightly together. 'I wanted to know why you needed to see her. It seemed rather odd that you'd come all the way from Cornwall merely to speak to her.'

'I told you,' he snapped. 'I happened to be in London. This was the kind of personal business which ought to be discussed face to face.'

If his profile weren't so grim, she might find her confession easier to make. Ethan had the knack of making her lose confidence rapidly and didn't seem to care sometimes whether he was charming or not. His mood unnerved her. Behind it lay a darkness of frightening intensity.

'You did,' she said tremulously. 'Discuss it, I mean. That is...' She stopped, alerted by the huge swell of his angry chest. 'Ethan——'

'I discussed it?' he asked tightly, a curious bitterness in his tone.

'Yes. With me. That is——'

She stiffened as his arm moved along the back of her seat and his big hand curled around her neck. Fear slid down Roxy's spine.

'Yes?' he prompted.

She licked her lips nervously. His long fingers climbed into her hair and he turned her head in his direction. She quailed at the glance he gave her, hostile, cold, piercing her heart like an icicle.

'Ethan——'

'Go on,' he grated.

'I'm Roxanne Page,' she said miserably. 'Roxy.' She waited for his explosion.

'I already knew that,' he said laconically.

Horror swept through her. 'You knew? But...when?' she asked, through white lips. 'At what stage did you realise?'

The car began to lose speed. He ignored her for a few minutes, concentrating on moving into the slow lane.

'Say something,' she begged.

His face set, he headed for the sliproad leading to a service station. There was a quality about his rigid body that disturbed her. It seemed more than a mere disappointment that she'd been evasive and played a silly game.

The whole of his body exuded a carefully controlled anger, from his hard, cold eyes to the harshly stabbing foot on the brake and accelerator. Roxy decided not to say anything in defence of herself while he was driving in this mood.

Eventually they drove off the motorway and he parked in the service area. A heavy silence weighed the air and Roxy felt herself tensing.

When did he know? Before his charming smile, the careful seduction, the hot kisses? She flung open the door, jumped out and took in huge gulps of cold night air, feeling physically sick. Embarrassment was hot on her body as every touch of his hands and his persuasive, lying words branded her with their mockery.

'You swine!' she whispered, into the darkness. He'd deliberately used her, knowing she was trying to wheedle information out of him, banking on the fact that whatever he did he'd get away with. Roxy felt she'd lost her dignity and had been totally humiliated.

Suddenly unable to stand, she returned to the seat, throwing her head back and fighting desperately to pull herself together.

'You're a calculating bastard,' she muttered through cold lips.

'And you?' he enquired sardonically. *'Bubbles?'*

She went hot. 'I'm sorry,' she mumbled.

'Oh. That makes it all right, then? I'm to forgive you for concealing your identity so that you could vamp me and discover why I'd called?'

'It wasn't quite like that,' she mumbled. 'I didn't mean you to react so forcefully.'

'It was,' he growled. 'And I was teaching you a lesson. I almost demanded my pound of flesh, you know, while we were still in your flat. I nearly opted for driving you crazy for me. But I had other things on my mind,' he said contemptuously.

'You wouldn't have been able to make me want you,' she snapped.

His hand snaked out and caught her face, half crushing her jaw in its grasp.

'Oh, yes, I would,' he snarled. 'I'm very determined, very ruthless, remember?'

His mouth bruised hers in a hard, punishing kiss. Its brutality made Roxy cringe. He released her in contempt and she sullenly fingered her swollen lips, feeling incensed. Ethan had pretended an interest he'd never felt.

'How did you know it was me?' she demanded.

Mockery touched his lips and eyes. 'You were too eager to be true,' he said. 'Too sexy, too willing. I'm attractive to women, but I'm not dynamite. I heard the shop assistant speak your name and thought I must have been hallucinating, because the little ruffian at the funeral couldn't have been the flashy, extrovert city girl who wiggled her hips at the slightest provocation. Then your secretary spoke. The telephone line had been poor, but I recognised his voice. *That* wasn't disguised. Your fake accent was, of course.'

'I was annoyed,' she defended herself. 'You'd been as friendly as an iceberg at the funeral. And you were in the wrong not to tell me you knew who I was.'

'And miss all the fun?' he drawled. 'No. It amused me to play along, waiting to find out why you were acting like Mata Hari. Or rather, Bubbles.'

'You took advantage of the situation,' she seethed. 'You tried to seduce me.'

'Why not?' he said harshly. 'It was enjoyable, despite the fact it was for other reasons than the physical. I knew exactly what I was doing. You fell for it all, didn't you?'

Roxy fumed. No one got the better of her. Until now. 'What were you hoping to achieve?' she asked coldly.

'Sense,' he said curtly. 'Why look like a refugee from a tramps' home at your own mother's funeral?'

'It was sunny when I left London. I arrived in pouring rain and had to borrow things from the inn-keeper,' she said wearily.

'You say you didn't set out to seduce me. What were you trying to do?' he barked.

'I told you. I was suspicious.'

'Liar!' His furious, barely controlled face was thrust close to hers. 'You scheming, devious, manipulating little bitch!'

Roxy's eyes widened in distress. 'What——'

He uttered an oath and cruelly pulled her around in the seat. He looked as if he was going to hit her, an expression of pure hatred on his face. 'I promise you this,' he hissed. 'If you've been laughing at me all along, I'll make you regret the day you ever tried to deceive Ethan Tremaine!'

That made Roxy angry. If he was furious because he'd discovered he'd been trying to seduce a working-class girl, then he was despicable.

'You *were* playing me along all the time, weren't you?' he asked through gritted teeth. 'You were bored and amusing yourself. Is that why you accepted my invitation to Carnock? To twist the knife? Hoping to make me hot for you? Then intending to fling your acquisition of land at me?' His eyes narrowed. 'Had Penhaligon phoned you?'

She stared at him in defiance. He wouldn't bully her.

'Yes. When I was out of my office, talking to Joe. What do you mean about the land?'

The grip on her shoulders tightened cruelly. She recoiled at the malevolence pouring from him, but was jerked forwards again till she could feel his fierce, ragged breath fanning her skin with its heat.

'You know something, don't you?' he spat, giving her a rough shake. 'What is it? What's in the will?'

'I don't know! Stop that!' she cried angrily, bracing herself against his chest.

'You do! Your mother was as scheming as you are,' he snarled. 'If I thought...' He flinched. 'If I thought for one moment that you had any claim on any part of my inheritance, I'd throw you out of the car. While it was moving.'

Fear and dismay made her bite her lip anxiously. He was exactly like Cain: filled with erupting violence.

'Be reasonable. There must be a small bequest to me if I've been invited down. I must be involved somehow,' she muttered.

Her chin was gripped tightly by his finger and thumb and her face tipped up to his. She stared, hypnotised by his coal-black, murderous eyes. How could so much hatred be sent from one person to another? she agonised. Her lower lip began to tremble.

'Don't try that,' he said contemptuously. 'It won't work. I don't think you can have any idea what I feel about you at this moment. And perhaps for your peace of mind it's just as well. Tell me honestly—did your mother speak of any legacy?'

'No. Only that . . .' She stopped, wishing she'd kept her mouth shut.

'Tell me,' he grated, jerking her chin up higher.

'You brute,' she whispered. 'You're hurting me.' The grip loosened slightly. 'Mother only said that Mrs Tremaine often threatened to disinherit you and your sister. She held a grudge against you. But Mother never told me if her threat had been carried out.'

She was flung back into her seat as Ethan released her, and he slowly resumed his position behind the driving wheel. Flicking a glance at him from under her lashes, she saw that he was staring hauntedly into space, his whole body utterly dejected.

'She wouldn't,' he muttered. 'She couldn't have written off generations of Tremaines like that. We've been at Carnock for centuries. We belong there.' His eyes closed in pain. 'It can't be true,' he grated through his teeth. 'I will never leave!'

'Maybe you won't have to——'

'Shut up,' he snarled. 'You've caused me enough hassle as it is. You won't say a word for the rest of the journey. It looks as if I'm stuck with you, temporarily. I'll find a bed for you tonight at Carnock and then you must sort yourself out. I don't want a seductive Jezebel defiling the place for any longer than necessary.'

'It didn't bother you before,' she snapped.

'I thought . . . *dammit*!' Violently he started up the car and drove off, his body pulsing with fury.

Roxy slumped in the seat, wishing the ground would swallow her up. She'd been in the wrong. He wasn't perfect, but that didn't excuse anything she'd done. Her sense of fun had led her astray and she longed to put the clock back. It had been a stupid thing to do. She'd tried to hide behind a false personality so that Ethan wouldn't hurt her with his sneering condescension, and she had been treated with even greater contempt as a result. She deserved it all.

But he should never have used the opportunity in the way he did. It had been a cheap way of showing how he despised her.

Now they had every reason to hate one another. How strange, the twists of Fate. Perhaps, after the will had been read and he felt certain of his hold on Carnock, he would be in a better mood. She could apologise properly and tell him that he had the wrong idea about her mother. It was a mystery why he thought Milly Page was a schemer.

It was a ghastly journey. Ethan wouldn't stop at all, and after five hours Roxy's head was buzzing from lack of food. She dreaded to think how he must be feeling, driving with a hard light in his eyes and his body absolutely screwed up with tension.

If only she could sleep! But the atmosphere was too highly charged with hostility, and Roxy felt as if she was on red alert.

They swept over the suspension bridge which crossed the River Tamar separating Devon from Cornwall. A few miles on, Ethan took a small turning down a narrow lane that twisted and turned for ages. Grass ran down the middle of the lane and high banks lined the sides. Driving slowly, twice he had to halt when first a badger and then a fox hurried in front of the car, picked out in the headlights.

Suddenly Roxy was flung to one side as Ethan swung into a driveway and stopped, leaving the engine running. Roxy saw a sign for Carnock House and looked across at Ethan. His breath exhaled and she noticed that his shoulders were set in a more relaxed position as he sat there. In the beams of the head-lights and the silvered moon, she could just make out an avenue of trees arching over the drive ahead. Fields on either side dropped to dark woods, and far away in the distance twinkled the lights of a farmhouse. Nervously Roxy realised that it was the only building in sight. Nothing else disturbed the solid darkness of the hills.

Slowly the car bumped down the drive beneath the black branches and eerily pale leaves. Then she saw lawns and shrubberies and the lights were picking out the stark whiteness of a huge stone house, which had been hidden by the dense mass of trees behind it.

Without a word, Ethan stopped the car in front of a massive Georgian entranceway and got out, stretching. Not knowing what to do, Roxy slid out too, glad to ease her cramped limbs.

The utter silence startled her. All her life she'd been used to the background of traffic. Here, there was nothing. Her ears pricked up. Just an owl, hooting. It sounded beautiful in the still night, yet plaintive.

'Go inside,' he said curtly. 'I'll bring your bag.'

'You'll need to unlock the door first,' she said.

He threw her a crushing look. 'This is Cornwall. You don't need to lock anything around here. In-cluding your bedroom door.'

Roxy felt the heat rise from her toes to her face, but she wouldn't let him bait her. One of them would walk away from all this with some dignity, she thought grimly.

She found the light switch inside the door, but her hand faltered and dropped lifelessly. A low, choking breath jerked from her lungs and she clutched blindly at the door-frame, unwilling to see any evidence of the fire which had killed her mother.

'What's the matter?' asked Ethan harshly, as he pushed past her and flooded the hall with light that penetrated through her closed lids. 'Now what are you playing at?'

'The fire——' she managed.

'Oh. I forgot you didn't know. It was confined to the far end, where the kitchen is,' he said gruffly. 'Your mother and mine had saved on heat and housework by shutting up most of the house. They slept in the sitting-room, next to the kitchen. I had the damaged west wing rebuilt completely.'

Roxy fought to regain control of herself, willing her trembling legs to move. When she opened her eyes wearily, she saw that he was looking at her sardonically.

'You loved your mother, then,' he said. 'I did wonder, when you dressed as you did and didn't bother to stay at the funeral.'

'What was the point?' she asked. 'I didn't know any of you and didn't want to. I got the impression that the feeling was mutual.'

His eyes were dark, remembering. 'I wasn't feeling kindly disposed to Milly Page's daughter. Your mother refused me access to my mother and turned her into a helpless, dependent and neurotic old lady. For that I hate her. You might as well know that.'

Under Roxy's astonished eyes, he picked up their bags and mounted the graceful oak staircase, taking its sweeping curves in huge strides. Roxy hurried after him.

'What are you talking about?' she cried vigorously. 'You can't possibly think that of my mother! She was the kindest, most caring——'

'Too kind, too caring,' he snapped, his long legs quickly covering the length of the landing. Roxy had to half run to keep up. 'You can have this room. It used to be a maid's bedroom. I'll bring some linen in.'

Roxy sank miserably on to the small, narrow bed. No maid had slept in there for years, judging by the musty, unused smell. She suddenly felt very lost and lonely, and so tired that she was incapable of moving. A scowling Ethan dropped a pillow, sheets and a blanket on to the bed and she didn't even move, but sat staring dumbly into space through spiky wet lashes. He paused, his face thunderous.

'Waiting for me to put you to bed?' he asked scathingly.

'You swine!' she whispered.

'I could,' he muttered thickly. 'Heaven help me, but I could!'

Her head turned slowly to look at him and, when she saw the naked but unwanted lust in his eyes, tears began to roll down her cheeks unchecked. This stupid misunderstanding was making them both unhappy. It had to stop.

'Ethan——' she began brokenly.

Her body was hauled upwards violently. His merciless kiss crushed her mouth so fiercely that she could feel the hardness of his teeth beneath his angry lips. It was as if he was trying vainly to eliminate any softness. Under his onslaught, her head fell back and the weight of his body arched her supple spine till she thought it would snap. Then she was released with such vehemence that she went flying on to the bed.

'I hate you!' he snarled. 'You and your mother will regret ever trying to harm my family!'

Incensed at the injustice, her tears dried by a storm of fury that overwhelmed her, Roxy flew at him in frustration. But he held her at arm's length and merely smiled infuriatingly. Realising she was getting nowhere, Roxy became still and tried to twist her wrists out of his painful grip.

'You're a bully, Ethan Tremaine,' she accused. 'You threaten and accuse me, kiss me and try to seduce me and use physical violence, all in the name of your precious family honour.'

There was a shrill scream from the garden outside and she jumped in terror, her blue eyes wide and questioning.

Ethan gave a mirthless laugh. 'A vixen,' he said softly. 'Very appropriate, mimicking your spitfire attack and yelling. Sleep well, if you can, with the creatures of the night calling to each other in the dark outside. If,' he added, his contemptuous eyes raking her taut body, 'you get lonely, don't come looking for me. Join them—go and howl at the moon and practise your witchcraft on the animals.'

The door slammed behind him. Dully, Roxy struggled through her tears and lethargy to make the bed, falling into it still in her luxurious white underwear. It was asking for trouble to sleep nude, as she normally did. Her eyes drooped, then closed, before her head hit the pillow and her tightly knotted muscles unfolded.

The birds woke her. For a long time she lay on her stomach, irritably thrashing her legs till the confining sheets were pushed away by her feet. A clear, piping call echoed out through the air. She listened drowsily as an astonishing variety of bird-song erupted in liquid notes. Then her skin tingled. She could also hear the imperceptible sound of breathing, in her room. Her head flipped to one side and she froze.

Ethan lounged against the open door, his face grim and his eyes crawling up her shapely calves, over her thighs and tight buttocks, bringing coursing fire into

Roxy's veins. Her body tried to melt as his slow gaze wandered with insolent appraisal up her half-naked back and paused on the expanse of pale gold flesh. His long black lashes fluttered in a mocking caress of the dainty bootlace strap which had slipped down over her shoulder. Roxy felt a trickle of warm desire and hated herself. Though she hated him more for causing it so effortlessly.

'Get out!' she grated. 'How dare you stand there and watch me sleep?'

'I came to rouse you,' he murmured.

'I'm awake.' Roxy had chosen one interpretation of the word. She hoped that was what he meant. It was a little early to be fighting him off.

'I want you to have breakfast and be out of here before I go to work.'

Furtively she felt for the bedclothes and rolled over. She frowned at him. He was dressed in faded green cords and a checked shirt, the sleeves rolled up to the elbow and displaying brawny arms. Roxy checked her watch and groaned. Six o'clock!

'This is an ungodly hour. Milking the cows, are you?' she asked scathingly.

'Get dressed. Down the stairs, turn left.'

She ate alone, feeling incongruous in the big country kitchen, wearing her most elegant primrose yellow linen suit. Its wide shoulders and cinched-in waist with a little flounce to the jacket made her hips look very slender, and her legs long and tanned. But she was out of place, and she knew it. The effect was quite intentional. She didn't want to fit. She didn't want to let his house delight her.

Ethan came in after a while, this time dressed in a smart city suit. He silently waited while she finished, then led her to his car.

'I'm fixing up a meeting with Penhaligon today,' he said curtly, flinging in her overnight bag. 'I don't want you hanging around till Monday. You can wait in the lounge at the village pub. I'll get a message to you when we're to meet. You'll be back in London tonight.'

It wouldn't be soon enough, she thought. As they moved slowly up the drive, her eyes lingered on the scene they left behind. The house glistened in the sun like sugar icing. In front, the beautifully kept lawn stretched lush and green. Ornamental trees and some enormous oaks interrupted the view. And that view, she had to admit, was stunning.

Carnock lay tucked into the gentle curve of a low hill. From the lawn, and with increasingly tantalising glimpses through the drive of trees, Roxy could see across a deep river valley to a series of hills.

Daffodils and bluebells vied for space on either side of the verge. Roxy couldn't prevent herself from looking in all directions, her head turning backwards and forwards in an effort not to miss anything.

'Yes,' said Ethan thoughtfully. 'Lovely, isn't it? And I'm not letting any of it go out of the family.'

She nodded. 'I don't blame you,' she said. 'It's like entering a lost world.'

He made no reply, and she was sorry when they left the estate and turned into the little lane.

The innkeeper at the Weary Friar remembered her, and brought her endless cups of coffee and the morning papers. Eventually, near midday, Ethan appeared and announced they were holding the meeting at the house in half an hour.

Annabel was already sitting in the bay window of a big sunny drawing-room, her face pinched and grey. When Roxy entered, Annabel's eyes narrowed and examined every detail of Roxy's elegant Italian suit.

Putting on a show of indifference, Roxy strolled over to one of the gilt chairs arranged in a semicircle in front of a turn of the century fruitwood desk and sat down nonchalantly.

Two men came in and spoke to the agitated Annabel, and Roxy could hear Ethan's deep voice soothing her.

'Miss Page? I'm John Penhaligon.'

She shook his hand, liking the fair-haired lawyer immediately. 'Will this take long?' she asked. 'The circumstances——'

'A little unusual, yes,' said John Penhaligon in a kindly tone. 'It's unfortunate that the will has only just been discovered. Mrs Tremaine drew it up herself. But it's perfectly legal. The signatures of delivery men are just as acceptable as those of anyone else.'

'How did it turn up?' asked Roxy.

'My sister found it in the attic,' said Ethan. 'It took us that long to get that far, the place was in such a mess.'

Roxy bristled at the intended slur on her mother's housekeeping abilities. She listened to the formal reading, acutely conscious of Ethan sitting next to her, his thighs only an arm's reach away. Uncomfortable, she shifted in her chair and crossed her legs with a whisper of silk. He drew in an enraged breath and she frowned. It hadn't been her intention to provoke him.

Distracted, she hadn't heard the last two sentences spoken by the lawyer. But Ethan's hands were gripping the edge of his chair and she quickly pulled her mind together, feeling a distinct chill in the atmosphere. Annabel seemed to be frozen like a statue, her mouth shaped in an astonished circle.

'What did you say?' grated Ethan, leaning forwards.

The lawyer cleared his throat. ' . . . so I leave all my worldly goods to my good friend and housekeeper, Milly Page.'

Roxy's mouth dropped open in shock and a warm feeling crept into her body. Mrs Tremaine must have formed a very high opinion of her mother and valued her services highly. How sad that she never knew. She waited for the solicitor to declare the will null and void, because her mother had died with Mrs Tremaine.

Everyone was very still, and it seemed as if Ethan was trying to set light to the hapless Mr Penhaligon with his blazing eyes.

'No!' Ethan breathed. 'It can't be true—you've read it wrongly! Not everything!'

'I'm sorry, Mr Tremaine, that's what it says.'

Ethan's agonised face tugged at Roxy's heart strings. How that must hurt him, she thought. His mother had rejected him cruelly. Still, it was all right in the end. The house was his. He had that small consolation.

'There's nothing else? She's not mentioned me or my sister at all?' asked Ethan, white-faced.

Roxy couldn't understand why he wasn't more pleased that there were no further clauses, or bequests. Mr Penhaligon had refolded the document in a purposeful manner.

'Only to explain the bit about your hostility to her,' said Mr Penhaligon in an embarrassed voice.

'Nothing?' he breathed, his eyes dark with shock. The lawyer gently shook his head. 'You're not mentioned.'

'No!' Annabel ran stumbling from the room and Ethan watched, too stunned to go after her. His hands shook on his knees.

Sensing she'd missed something vital, Roxy finally found her voice. 'Surely the will doesn't apply?' she asked tremulously. 'My mother died in the fire, too. So that means——'

'Roxanne,' said Mr Penhaligon, 'it wasn't possible to determine the time of death precisely for either your mother or Mrs Tremaine. In such circumstances, it is deemed in law that the younger woman died last. In this case, the younger woman was your mother. As you can see, officially she inherited Carnock House and the estate. You are her only living relative. There's no doubt. Carnock is yours.'

Numbed, she swayed in her chair, a coldness freezing her body.

'The hell it is!' exploded Ethan, jumping from his chair, his fists clenched. 'That will was made under pressure. Why else would Milly Page persuade my mother to get in strange lawyers? Why else would my mother deny her own blood?' He whirled around to face Roxy, his face working in rage. 'I'll fight this, every inch of the way. Carnock is mine by rights, *mine*! Every stone of this building, every tree, down to the last damn blade of grass!'

'There is a doctor's certificate attesting to the satisfactory state of Mrs Tremaine's mind,' said John Penhaligon sternly. 'You are of course entitled to contest the will on the grounds of undue influence. However, in view of your mother's remarks about the hostility existing between you, I'd advise you to accept the inevitable, Ethan.'

'Never,' he muttered. 'Not while there's breath in my body! I'll contest it. By heaven, I will! Milly Page wheedled her way into my mother's confidence and stopped anyone from visiting. She made my mother totally dependent. I'll take this to the highest court in the land, if necessary. I've lost this house once; I *won't* lose it again.'

Roxy stared at his anguished face in distress.

'You're wrong about my mother——' she began.

'No, I'm not,' he snarled. 'And I'll prove it. I'll drag her name through the dirt if I have to, but I'll prove it. There's only one way you can prevent me, and that's by selling outright, now. Well?'

Quivering with indignation at his vicious attack on her mother, Roxy rose smoothly and met his eyes in a bold stare.

'Mrs Tremaine told my mother many stories about you,' she said quietly. 'But I never fully believed them until now. She said you were domineering and cruel, heartless and vindictive. Your conduct recently has convinced me that's true. And because of that, and the scurrilous slander about my mother, I'm not prepared to do anything to make your life easier. I keep Carnock.'

'What do you know about running a place like this?' he seethed. 'It's not your style, you as much as admitted it. All those pixies and pasties,' he mocked. 'How the hell are you going to run your business and Carnock? Who takes over the grass keep? And the management of the white heather plantation? How soon will you be bored with this slow country bumpkin life, Roxanne?'

'What I do is none of your business,' she snapped, slightly daunted by what he said. Her life was too full to take on such a commitment. He was right; it sounded as if she'd need to sell up pretty quickly. But one thing was for sure: Mrs Tremaine and her mother had been firmly opposed to Ethan living here, and that was good enough for Roxy. She'd do everything she could to stop him from getting his hands on the house.

Whatever it cost her. Inwardly she shrank at the vindictiveness in his expression.

'I'll make it my business,' he said in soft menace. 'Believe me, in everything you do, you'll come up against me. Nothing is going to stop me. Nothing.'

Roxy flinched at the vehemence of his tone and his harshness. She felt bewildered and very alone. Ethan loathed her. She wanted to cry.

CHAPTER FIVE

EVERY bone and sinew aching from the tense way she held her body, Roxy dropped exhausted into her chair. The lawyer explained the legal procedure to her, but she was barely listening, incapable of understanding what had happened.

Ethan had become very still and seemed in perfect control now, even his breathing more regular than hers. The man had a will of iron.

'It would be better,' suggested John Penhaligon, 'if this feud was ended. Neighbours should never be at daggers drawn.'

'No, they shouldn't,' agreed Ethan softly, and Roxy knew from the hardness underlying his words that he wasn't going to kiss and make up. 'You know my feelings about this place, John. Impress them on her.'

'Where are you going, Ethan?' asked the lawyer, seeing he was striding out of the room. 'There are a number of legal points to tie up——'

'I'm going to see Annabel,' he said bleakly.

Roxy turned distressed eyes to John Penaligon. 'What shall I do?' she asked.

'I can't advise you,' he answered. 'Ethan is my client. Speak to your own solicitor and perhaps one or two of your friends. I'll finish off the arrangements, shall I?'

Roxy nodded and tried to absorb all the information. But the reality of owning a large country estate hadn't yet sunk in. She looked at the maps, her head spinning. Gifts like this didn't land in your lap, out of the blue. You had to slog away to win anything; only by the sweat of your brow did you get anywhere. This was impossible to believe.

Penhaligon gave her a sheaf of documents and his business card, then left. Roxy decided to ring Joe. She explained what had happened and was upset by his raucous laughter.

'It's not funny, Joe,' she said, hurt.

'It is,' he chortled. 'Now, be sensible. Stop fooling around——'

'I'm *not* fooling! Everything I've said is true!' she cried. 'And I've no idea when I'll be back. There's so much to do here.'

'Do? In the country? Like...buy wellington boots?'

He went into another bout of laughter and Roxy began to fume. It wasn't that amusing. Everyone seemed to think she was only fitted for tripping around expensive restaurants and sitting at a desk. She gave Joe a few stilted instructions and rang off.

She wandered to the full-length window and looked out with dazed eyes at the lush emerald lawn. On either side, the ornamental shrubs and herbacious border looked very neat. Ethan must have done quite a lot in the time he'd been here. Blossom trees dropped tiny petals on to the carpets of primroses and blue-bells beneath the trees which swept down beside the drive.

The scene brought a smile to her face. When Ethan entered, he brought her back to earth again by scowling at the sight of her contented face, and then he retreated behind his cold mask. He was cradling a glass of whisky, and when her eyes rested on it he gestured sardonically with it.

'Hope you don't mind,' he drawled. 'My whisky, your glass.'

'This isn't easy for me, either,' she said quietly.

'No. And it'll get worse. Annabel has gone to bed with a bottle of sleeping pills. We'll get out as soon as she feels able. *For now.* Do you want lunch?' She shook her head. 'Then I'll walk you round the boundary.'

Roxy blinked. 'What? Why——'

'I want to make absolutely sure you don't come on to Tremaine Farm—my land,' he said coldly. 'Find something suitable to wear. I'll be waiting outside.'

All she had was a shocking-pink towelling top and jeans. Quickly she changed, and pulled on a pair of trainers. When she found Ethan, he was staring up at a giant-sized tree on the lawn. Unseen, she watched him for a moment. It looked as if he'd been born to roam the countryside. In his faded cords, black boots and easy shirt, his hair tousled by the breeze, he stood as still and silent as the tranquil woods, as proud as the towering tree above him. Whereas she felt, and looked, wrong. That annoyed her.

Of course she'd feel an interloper on her own land. But that would alter, after a while. Though, she mused, Ethan would always look incomparably *right*. Then she remembered. She was intending to sell.

'It's a lovely tree,' she ventured. If they were going on a long walk, they might as well be civilised.

'It's dying,' he said shortly.

'Oh.' She looked up. 'It's got leaves.'

He threw her a withering look. 'I give it ten years.'

'That's ages!' she cried, surprised.

'In its life span that's no time at all. This redwood is over a hundred years old. There's a lot of dead wood and those lower branches are dangerous. And that Monterey over there,' he jabbed with his finger at a huge spreading pine, with deeply ridged bark, 'it needs dead-wooding too, and the split branch cut out.'

'Why didn't you do that?' she asked, running to keep up with his big strides. 'You've been here since November.'

'I told you.' He frowned. 'The house was almost derelict and the grounds a vast wasteland. I've worked miracles in the last few months. Don't criticise me for things I haven't got around to yet. I had to choose my priorities. And I needed to spend time with Annabel, too.'

'I'm sorry,' she apologised. 'But if Mrs Tremaine was well off, why didn't she spend money on keeping the place going properly? And surely my mother didn't like chaos?'

'My mother, if you remember, had been turned into a recluse,' he said tightly, frowning as he touched a swathe of ivy, creeping up the trunk of a tree. 'No one came here. No one set foot on Carnock apart from the delivery men.' He pulled a pair of secateurs out of his pocket. 'You'll have to cut this ivy off each tree. From down low... to about here. Every piece.'

Roxy's eyes widened. 'You're making that up!' she cried. 'You're trying to make me believe there's more work than there really is! No one could take out all the ivy on every tree——'

'It has to be done,' he said doggedly. 'If you don't believe me, get a second opinion. Roxy, you're not dealing with short-term actions and decisions now,' he added, sounding exasperated. 'These trees need to breathe. Maybe the ivy looks pretty. Maybe the trees look healthy. In ten, twenty, thirty years, they won't be. You do a bit at a time. It's a long-term operation. You're preserving for the future.'

She was silent, casting her eye around, a little daunted by the Herculean task. Ivy straggled up every tree, it seemed. She had no option but to sell. If she tried to keep the house on with a manager and housekeeper, she'd also need a gardener. That would stretch her resources too far. John Penhaligon had said that the income from Mrs Tremaine's investments would pay for the upkeep of the house and land, but wasn't quite enough to support her if she stopped working. Not that she wanted to, of course.

They moved up a track, the spring sun warm on their faces. She stopped in pleasure when she found a bank of violets, their dark indigo flowers backed by a froth of white. The scent was unmistakable.

'Is that garlic?' she asked Ethan, her nose wrinkling.

'Ransom. Wild garlic. Come and see the orchard behind,' he said shortly.

It seemed to Roxy that he had become angrier and more tense. He pushed through an overgrown gap and she had to struggle through on her own, getting caught up in thorny brambles.

'Ow!' she cried, examining her hands. Red bumps were appearing on them and they stung like mad.

'Nettles are difficult to eradicate from the ground,' he said.

'They would be.' Roxy glared. The work here was mounting up, and he didn't have to take a delight in rubbing that fact in. Then she looked up.

'Oh, Ethan!' she beamed, forgetting their antagonism and catching his arm. 'What a beautiful sight!'

Before her were rows and rows of gnarled old trees, thick with lichen, their branches bowed down with delicate blossom. She ran through the long grass beneath, down the avenues, and whirled around at the end. She owned an orchard! Her own apples, pears...

Eagerly she ran up to him. 'Tell me what they are,' she begged. He stepped back, his eyes pained.

'They're ruined,' he growled, turning his back on her.

Roxy ran around him and planted her feet apart, folding her arms in an attitude of immovability.

'I know what you're doing,' she snapped. 'You're trying to put me off——'

'I'm telling you the truth!' he snarled. 'The whole of the estate is badly run down. When will you get that into your thick head? Do you think I like seeing it spoilt? It twists my gut every time I walk around.'

'It just needs good management,' she said firmly. 'I can run a business; I can run land.'

'For pity's sake!' he exclaimed in exasperation. 'You have to know what needs doing first. An ignorant manager is no good, you must realise that, in any business. Here, you have to look ahead as well and plan for the distant future. Replanting, for instance, growing new trees to replace the old ones before they die, and staggering the replacements every three, five, ten years, so in fifty or a hundred years' time some poor devil isn't left with a bare landscape. Planning for posterity is essential. You don't only consider your lifetime, but those of your descendants. Ever think of that?'

Miserably she shook her head. 'I'll learn,' she said stubbornly.

'You'd better,' he said, giving her a jaundiced look and walking on.

They mounted a bank and below them was spread a series of hills, rolling down to a wood. Small, dark hedges divided the fields, each one a different colour, ranging from the dark red earth to palest green. Roxy laid her hand on the flaking bark of a tall Scots pine, seeing for the first time its multiple colours. A sense of peace came over her. Living here would be very restful, she mused, stroking the tree. A pheasant croaked nearby and she smiled.

'I want to learn,' she said softly.

Ethan sighed. 'You've got too much ground to make up. And a way of thinking and living that's all wrong. Take the specimen trees, for example, and the way each generation has to make a contribution for the future. It's a world away from your throw-away society, Roxy. I've never asked anyone for a favour before, but I'm asking you now. Don't even *think* of being an absentee landowner. You'll destroy Carnock. It deserves better than that. I'd rather you sold to anyone than put in a manager without supervision.'

She shifted uncomfortably. He was right. 'Have you decided not to contest the will?' she asked.

'No. But that'll take a long time. I can wait, Roxy. I just don't want to take over a derelict house and land which hasn't been worked with an eye to the future.'

Her eyes scanned the drifts of bluebells, which made the fields ahead look like hazy sky.

Generations, she thought, her face serious. If I plant trees, people who haven't even been born yet will walk under them one day. Or have picnics in their shade, make love beneath them, or just look.

'It's very tempting,' she said slowly. 'So lovely.'

Her eyes closed and the sun glowed on her up-turned face. A faint scent of wild honeysuckle wafted on a light breeze and suddenly she found she was listening, really listening, for the first time. Leaves rustled. There was a tractor, far away. Bees droned. A small bird trilled nearby, putting its whole heart into an agonisingly sweet song.

'You were right,' she breathed, feeling all her body relax. 'Even a townie like me can appreciate the quality of life here.'

She turned to Ethan and saw he watched her closely. Her emotions were tugged by the longing in his eyes. No wonder he wanted Carnock; no wonder he desired it above all things. Sympathetically, she reached out her hand.

He jerked away, out of reach. 'Don't touch me!' he muttered.

'I only wanted to say that I understood your feelings,' she whispered.

'Oh, do you? Then you'll understand this,' he said savagely, taking her by the shoulders in a grip of steel. His mouth ground cruelly on hers and then she was released, gasping.

'Why do you do that?' she asked miserably. Kisses ought to bring pleasure, not a pain that sliced through her heart. 'Are you trying to prove there's one area at least where you can dominate me? I know that already. You're stronger than I am physically. You don't have to prove it over and over again.'

'Why not?' he drawled. 'Why shouldn't I fight you with everything I have at my disposal? I told you I was ruthless.'

'I see. No holds barred,' she said quietly.

His eyes glittered and a smile of mockery crept to his lips. 'No quarter,' he murmured.

It took nearly three hours to complete the tour of the estate, and Roxy was exhausted and hungry when they returned to the house. Her head reeled, too, from the information he'd listed with a smugness that had been infuriating. One of her problems was that Ethan was taking away the livestock, and she would have to find cattle or sheep to eat the grass, otherwise it would become a wilderness again.

Depressed, she made herself a sandwich. Ethan had taken some food up to Annabel and was eating with her. Roxy felt very lonely and rather lost. What on earth was she going to do? Joe wouldn't be much help, nor would her friends. They would all think like him:

that it was hilarious she should even *be* in the country, let alone consider living there.

Of course she had to sell. She had her business to run, the one she'd lavished her love and affection on, and which was now just taking off. Roxy wandered out on to the terrace and absently watched a large black bird fly over with a bundle of twigs in its beak. It landed on the branch of a tree and disappeared into a hole.

She really must go to the library and find a book which would tell her what these birds were. Roxy frowned. There wasn't much point if she was leaving.

First she needed to make plans, and that meant she'd want paper and a pencil. Shrinking from asking a favour from Ethan, she decided to look around the house and see if she could lay her hands on something suitable.

Her fingers stroked the highly polished wood of the oak banister, revelling in its glass-like finish. Not only her mother, but generations of women had polished that. Looking with the eyes of possession, she saw every detail. There were the fraying curtains, the rotting wood in a windowsill, and the crowded knick-knacks of a typical Victorian collector. In the big main bedroom, the telephone was the only modern item. Dreamily she traced the linenfold panelling of the four-poster bed and laid her cheek against its velvet curtain.

'Roxy.'

She jumped and lifted startled eyes to Ethan. 'I was looking for some paper. And a pencil.'

'In here? My mother's room?'

'I was only looking around.'

'Surveying your prize.'

She made a denial with her head. 'Don't be angry with me,' she said. 'That's unjust——'

'Unjust, is it?' he growled. 'You, no relation of any kind to the Tremaines, take possession of this house by unfair, devious means, and you complain that my anger is unjust? Ye gods, Roxy, you want the world, don't you?'

'There's no point in talking to you,' she said dejectedly, walking towards the door.

He caught her arm and stopped her. Remembering the way he'd held out against her struggles before, she waited patiently until he became bored with trying to bully her.

'Are you going to make this your bedroom?' he asked tightly.

'What if I am?' she defied. 'It's my house, I can do what I like.'

'Bitch!' he swore. 'I don't want to think of you here.'

She lifted a mocking eyebrow. 'Is this sentimentality, or do you think I ought to confine myself to the servants' quarters?' she asked coldly.

Fear tingled along her spine at the way he looked at her.

'You appear to have the morals of a slut, ready to sell your body in exchange for information,' he snarled at her, tightening his grip. 'Women like you don't belong here.'

'I wasn't going to let you make love to me,' she said with a frosty glance. 'In fact, I find your touch repulsive.'

Roxy was lying. The movement of his thumb on the soft inner part of her arm was slowly insinuating itself into her vulnerable body. If she didn't escape from his grasp soon, or insult him so much that he let her go in disgust, she wouldn't be able to keep her breath even, and he'd know she was finding his touch pleasurable.

'How much longer are we going to stand here?' she asked in a bored tone. 'This doesn't serve any purpose. You really are behaving in a very tiresome way.'

His eyes darkened, and for a moment Roxy saw the hidden power of his anger within. She'd underestimated her own danger. His thumb circled her flesh till her whole body seemed focused on that one spot.

'I want you,' he said softly.

'You want Carnock, Ethan,' she said. 'Not me.'

'I want both.'

Somehow she managed to laugh, her head tilting to one side in an arrogant challenge that told him she wasn't afraid.

'Pity. You're not having either of them,' she said with a smile.

'Oh, yes, I am,' he said quietly. 'Because soon you'll want me too, and I don't intend that you'll ever spend a day without thinking about me, or needing me.'

The blade of pleasure knifed through her body at his passionate tone. Ethan was so arrogant, so sure of her. He'd go on, and on, till he forced her to admit she found him fascinating.

'I thought I was melodramatic,' she said sarcastically. 'You'd win prizes in an old time music hall play. I'm immune to you—especially now I know how you've behaved, especially after you insulted my mother's name, and particularly now I'm aware that you crave sex, pure and simple.'

'Not pure,' he said, pulling her back against the hard male warmth of his body. She froze instantly. 'Not simple,' he whispered savagely, twisting her around and imprisoning her. 'Not immune,' he growled deep in his throat, his mouth whispering in a tortuous path over her collarbone.

Her brief, sensual memories of him were instantly reawakened. To prevent herself from melting against him, she had to grit her teeth hard and keep her eyes open, even though they wanted to close. She stared at the picture on the opposite wall, forcing her brain to register its detail.

Ethan's lips ran over her throat, then feathered along her jaw.

'Do hurry up,' she sighed. 'I'm getting a backache, standing here like this.'

She kept her eyes looking as bored as possible, and wandering over the picture in a world-weary manner. His hand caught the back of her head and forced it around so that she had no choice but to look at him. His eyes were blistering.

'You're strong, Roxy,' he grated. 'But I'm stronger.'

'Not more he-man stuff,' she complained petulantly. 'If you bruise my arms, I'll have to take you to court on a charge of assault.'

Ethan shocked her with the muttered oath that flew from his lips.

'Give me one good reason why I shouldn't wring your damned neck,' he seethed.

'Because Carnock would revert to the state?' she hazarded.

He stiffened. 'You cold bitch,' he whispered.

'Incapable of accepting rejection?' she taunted.

'I'm wondering why I ever bother with women who don't know the meaning of——' He broke off. 'You win, for now,' he said, his fingers unwinding from her arm.

'Correction,' she said, inspecting the skin for signs of damage. 'I win, period. Admit you're defeated, Ethan. Go back to your nice new house and forget your dreams of living here.'

He smiled sourly. 'No quarter,' he repeated.

Roxy watched him go and let out a sigh of relief when the door closed softly behind him. Her own reactions had been bewildering and muddled. She understood his love of the house and why he was so determined not to lose it, and that sympathy was interfering with the way she ought to be slapping him down when he tried to make a pass.

But ... she couldn't deny that she found him exciting and that she enjoyed being kissed by him. Roxy wasn't inexperienced, and had no hang-ups about men. Yet instinctively she knew the feelings he aroused were quite different from any she'd experienced before. They made her want to know him better, to develop the highly charged physical attraction into more of a friendship.

While he was set on seducing and dominating her, that was impossible. She had to keep him at a distance.

It was a while before she decided to stop worrying about Ethan and continue her exploration of the house.

Basically, she decided, it was in fair repair, though she'd seen some worrying damp patches. When she found something to make her notes, she wandered around, jotting down everything that occurred to her. A survey was the first thing, maybe some essential repairs, then the estate agents could be called in.

She stopped by a window. The black bird was still stuffing twigs into that tree. Perhaps she'd go to the library this afternoon. There wasn't much else she could do, she was too tired from the walk that morning to do anything else apart from sit around, and with Ethan in the house she felt inhibited.

He was in the hall, buying fish from a man with a van outside, and she thumbed through the telephone directory, looking for a local taxi service.

'What do you want?' he asked ungraciously, when he saw what she was doing.

'A taxi,' she said coldly.

'Where to? The station?'

'Don't raise your hopes,' she told him sweetly. 'I'm going to Plymouth.'

'It'll cost the earth. I'll drive you there,' he said. 'Let me put this fish in the fridge first.'

'I want to go alone,' she said stiffly, flicking through the pages.

'Shopping, I suppose,' he muttered. 'The way you spend, there'll be nothing left of my mother's money by the time my claim is upheld.'

'What a good idea,' she said. 'I hadn't thought of that. And I was thinking of a trip to the library. Now I might change my mind and do a bit of shopping instead.'

'Library?' he mocked. 'You?'

'Since I'm going to be here for ages and ages,' she said, 'I thought I might learn the names of some of the birds on my land. In my garden. Nesting in my trees.'

'Don't push your luck,' he grated. 'I've got the message. It's emblazoned on your forehead in ten-foot letters and branded on my heart.'

She smiled faintly and began to dial a number. Ethan banged his hand down and cut her off.

'I have plenty of bird books,' he said. 'Borrow them.'

'There weren't any when I walked around the house,' she said, suspiciously. 'No library, no books.'

'Most of them are being rebound and repaired,' he said with a frown. 'Some I put in my own library in Tremaine House, where they can be kept properly. The others are in my bedroom upstairs. You didn't go in there, did you?'

Hearing voices, Roxy had avoided two upstairs rooms. She shook her head.

'I'll get them in a minute.' He went into the kitchen and Roxy heard the fridge door open and shut. She wandered to the window just in time to see a beautiful cock pheasant strolling across the lawn, and then looked up, hearing a seagull.

'Hear that cry?' asked Ethan, coming up behind her.

She chose to ignore the fact that he was crowding her. 'The seagull. Where is it?'

He snorted. 'Buzzard. It has a thinner, shorter cry, like a cat's mew. Look, there it is.'

Roxy gazed in awe. There were three buzzards, in fact, drifting on the wind without wingbeats, huge, and with an impressive ability to remain still in mid-air. She turned to say something to Ethan but he'd gone, and she felt disappointed not to be able to share her pleasure. Though, she thought wistfully, perhaps it was just as well. He returned and thrust a bird book into her hands and she went out on to the terrace, making so many identifications that she wasn't sure she could remember them all.

The big black one nesting in the tree was a jackdaw, and now that she looked carefully it had a grey head. She read about its habits, absorbed.

'I'm amazed you're not bored,' observed Ethan. 'You've been sitting there for nearly three hours.'

Roxy glanced at her watch and looked up, her eyes shining with discovery, but he looked away, plainly not interested in her new-found knowledge. He knew it all, of course, she thought resentfully, and her sparkle diminished.

'Annabel and I have had an early supper. We're going out for a while,' he said abruptly. 'We don't have any milk. If you want any before morning, you'll have to get it yourself.'

'I'm not too good at milking cows,' she said sarcastically.

He threw some keys into her lap. 'You can have my other car. Up the drive, turn left, first barn on the left. You'll find milk in there. In bottles,' he added drily. 'Leave the money.'

'People are very trusting round here,' she said after his retreating back.

He ignored her. Roxy gave a sigh, collected her purse and went to the garage. His second car turned out to be an ancient estate. Nervously she drove it up the driveway and in the direction he'd mentioned. The twisty lane had several completely blind bends, and she hooted the horn several times. It was also very narrow, though it was a pleasure to have bluebells and white stitchwort brushing each side of the car. Roxy felt pleased that she'd identified the dainty white flower. She picked up the milk, astonished to see so much money lying openly on a table in the barn, and started back.

A flash of yellow distracted her for a moment, and set her wondering if it might be a yellowhammer. She didn't have time to hoot as she rounded a particularly sharp bend.

Roxy gasped aloud at the sight of a huge tractor bearing down on her. She stamped hard on the brakes, but the tractor kept on coming. Bristling with indignation, she didn't stop to argue with the driver, but flung the gears into reverse.

It wasn't easy. The narrowness of the lane meant that she kept misjudging the distance, and scraping the side of the car. Then she saw to her horror that the tractor driver had gained on her and appeared to have every intention of shunting her backwards forcibly.

CHAPTER SIX

FRANTICALLY Roxy fought to control the car and signal to the man at the same time. Her quickly flashed glances told her that he was extraordinarily muffled for such a warm April evening. A chill crept into her stomach. It couldn't be intentional . . .

Gulping, she prayed she'd reach the entrance to the barn before he hit her. There was a crunch as the huge tractor wheels ground into the bumper, and then, as her horrified eyes locked on the driver, he began mercifully to reverse.

Roxy sat trembling.

'Scuse me, miss?'

She whipped her head around to see a cheerful farmer peering into the car.

'Mind moving along a bit, so I can get my heifers along?'

Roxy followed his jerking head and saw a herd of cows bearing down on her. That would be more than she could take! Nodding dumbly, she drove off down the road, her hands hardly able to hold the wheel.

Her teeth gritted in concentration. The man in the tractor would have had a view over the high hedges, and seen the cattle approaching. That was why he'd backed off.

She turned thankfully into the drive of Carnock House, acknowledging the farmer's shout of thanks with a weak wave. Either the incident with the tractor had been a local man carrying out some private vendetta against strangers, or . . .

The nausea rose up inside her. Roxy carefully parked the car in the garage and went indoors, pouring herself a drink.

Ethan had told her to get the milk. He'd told her where to go, given her the keys to his car. He'd known where she would be.

She paced up and down. It couldn't be true. He wouldn't play such a risky game. *No quarter.* Her head lifted and she stared, unseeing, into space.

Ethan was late. Roxy had waited up for him, but finally decided to go to bed. Typically, that was when he turned up. Disregarding her scanty covering—the shortie towelling robe over an even shorter nightie—she thundered down the stairs, far too angry to contemplate any sexual danger. He couldn't do anything with Annabel beside him.

However, when she saw he was alone she stopped in confusion.

'Well, well, well,' he drawled, running his eyes lasciviously over her body. 'What a welcome for a man to come home to!'

'What do you know about tractors in that lane?' she hurled, stabbing the air with a pointing finger and hoping it was in the right direction.

'Oh, parlour games,' he grinned, his white teeth flashing. 'Umm . . . they're red, big, noisy——'

'You know what I mean!' she yelled. 'The ones which smash into me when I'm driving——'

'What?' he roared, checking her up and down. 'My car——'

'Your *car*? What about me?'

'You look all right,' he glowered. 'Aren't you?'

'Physically, yes,' she snapped. 'But it took two good gins before I felt emotionally recovered.'

'Drunk again, are you?' he murmured.

'No, I'm not. Well, what about the tractor? Are you trying to intimidate me?'

'With a tractor?' He laughed. 'I can think of better ways than that.'

Still grinning, he took a few steps towards her and she backed away, seething.

'Leave me alone,' she raged. 'You tried to have me killed——'

'Don't be ridiculous. You'd better tell me about this tractor.'

He listened to her story with a weary smile, and then went to check his car.

'Did the tractor hit you on each side, too?' he enquired laconically, when he came back.

'No.'

His eyebrow rose fractionally. 'Then the dents in the coachwork are your doing? Perhaps,' he added coldly, 'as the crushed bumper is? Are you trying to pin the blame on someone else for your bad driving?'

'I tell you, the man intended to frighten me, to cause an accident,' she said doggedly.

'I want my car repaired and no more stupid tales,' he growled.

Roxy realised he wasn't going to offer any sympathy. She flung him a haughty look and stalked up the stairs.

'Very nice,' came Ethan's voice. 'Beautiful thighs.'

Her ribcage rose in outrage at his mocking laugh. Swine! she thought viciously.

Despite what he'd said, she locked her bedroom door. The locals might be trustworthy, but she didn't include Ethan in that generalisation. She slept well in the big bed, worn out by the events of the day and the country air.

As before, she woke to bird-song. That was the next thing to do, she smiled. She'd get one of those records so she could identify each one as it began to sing.

When she went downstairs, wearing the same jogging suit as the day before, she found a note telling her that Annabel had gone back to live in Tremaine House the night before and Ethan had gone to work.

Wonderful! She was alone! Roxy cut huge slabs of bread and spread them liberally with honey, then ate them outside on the terrace, which was already warm with the morning sun.

Soon after, she took pleasure in walking alone, knowing no one would disturb her. Her fingers learnt the different tree barks; she found fragrant wild honeysuckle clambering through an old magnolia tree and a tangle of dog roses, a riot of pure white blooms.

Happily, a gentle serenity slowing her normally darting movements, she picked wild flowers till she could carry no more.

But when she began to walk back to the house she began to notice that the ground had been churned up at the top of the lawn. Frowning, she pushed her way through the shrubbery and saw to her horror that a herd of cows was trampling over the grass!

Roxy cringed and dashed back into the bushes, taking a different route to the front door, but to her frustration it wouldn't open, even though she shook and rattled it violently in her anxiety.

The cows looked awfully near. If they *were* cows. She couldn't see any udders. Oh, no! she breathed, her mouth dry with fear. They were bulls. Bullocks. Whatever you called them.

She had to keep her head. There was a back entrance. Quickly she darted for that, but it was jammed, too. Roxy began to panic. There was only one door left, the terrace door, which she'd opened that morning and hadn't locked again. Cautiously she peered around the corner of the house. The young bulls were grazing contentedly on the roses, in the front border of the terrace. She'd have to be pretty quick to rush in and not be caught. Nervously Roxy eyed their horns. At least they weren't fully formed yet, she consoled herself.

She took a few deep breaths, and ran. The bullocks backed a little, startled, and she took advantage of their surprise to lunge for the handle of the door and wrenched at it. Only it didn't open.

'Ohh! Please open! Please, please!' she begged.

There was a clatter behind her, of hoof on stone. Roxy froze, apart from her breathing which seemed to accelerate. Imperceptibly she turned her head and saw that one of the bulls had wandered on to the terrace and was heading straight for her. With a bellow, it lowered its head and Roxy shook the door-handle wildly, screaming for it to open.

Within seconds, she was surrounded by the animals: hemmed in, petrified with terror and totally paralysed. She didn't dare to move a muscle. At the moment the bulls weren't threatening her, only trying to crush her. One or two reached out with huge thick tongues and licked at her body, and she felt the rasp with an inner shudder.

She didn't know how long she stood, plastered against the door, making herself as thin as possible, only that when she heard the sound of a car she could have fainted from relief.

'Hey, hey, hey!'

'*Ethan!*' she whispered through unmoving lips, watching hysterically as the cows moved away from her.

'What . . . Roxy! What the hell are you doing?' he yelled.

Her mouth dropped wide open.

'Move aside,' he said roughly. 'I'll have to phone for help. I'll never get these damn animals off that grass without help.'

'The door won't open,' she breathed, choking with disbelief. How callous could the man get?

Ethan frowned at her and tried it.

'I told you,' she said, trembling violently. 'It's jammed. I've been out here for hours and hours, pinned to the door by those big brutes. Damn you! Don't you care I've escaped death from goring or trampling by pure good fortune?'

He stopped trying the handle and looked at her in astonishment. Then he began to laugh. He roared till his head rolled back and he grew weak. Roxy bit her lip so the tears didn't come, though they welled up traitorously into her big blue eyes.

Seeing this, he tried to control himself. 'Roxy,' he grinned, 'it's a classic, I know, but they're not bulls.'

'They are! They don't have udders,' she said defiantly. She knew *something* about the country, she wasn't a complete fool.

'Roxy,' he laughed, 'they're heifers. That's cows who haven't had calves yet.'

'They threatened me——'

'They're curious. They love people. A shout or a clap of your hands would have made them back off,' he said gently. Then a broad grin spread over his face again. 'I'm sorry,' he said, helplessly, 'but your ignorance is very funny.'

Her lower lip trembled infuriatingly. 'I couldn't get in,' she said in a small voice. 'I was frightened.'

Ethan's arms folded around her. 'It's all right. I'm here now. The heifers can't hurt you, providing you don't decide to dive under their hooves. Come on, let's go in and we'll get you settled, then I'll try to shift them. Though I fear they're in love with my lawn. Your lawn,' he amended, with a small frown.

He twisted the handle, then grew still. 'There's glue around the outside,' he said in astonishment.

Roxy gave him a puzzled look, then bent to examine the door. A chill ran down the back of her neck.

'I couldn't get in the front door or the back one, either,' she said in a whisper.

'Sure?'

'Absolutely,' she nodded.

Ethan drew the parasol from the slot in the garden table and drove it straight through the window, using it to ease out the broken glass so that he could raise the sash. He helped Roxy inside without saying a word, pushed her into the kitchen and made her a cup of tea.

'I'm going to ring for a couple of men to come and drive the cows back to the pasture, and then I'm checking the other doors. All right?' he asked.

'Yes, thank you. Ethan—what's going on? Someone is trying to unnerve me, I know.'

'I doubt anyone would go to those lengths,' he said reassuringly. 'I'm sure it's all a coincidence.'

'The door?' she asked, her eyes huge in her pale face.

Ethan's hand stroked her hair in a light gesture, and Roxy longed to fling herself into his comforting and safe arms.

'A practical joke,' he said. 'Some young lad has discovered the potential of Superglue and is testing it on Carnock.'

'I'm afraid of what might happen next,' she said tremulously.

'Drink up,' he said in a falsely jolly voice. 'This is part of the joy of living in the country.'

She put her cup down with a bang. 'You didn't plan all this, did you?' she asked.

'What the hell are you talking about?' he cried. 'Do you imagine I'd let heifers in to ruin my lawn? It'll take a season to get the grass back to its former state. And I wouldn't glue up the doors. They'll probably have to be taken out of their frames. They're beautiful Georgian doors, damaged beyond repair.'

'But that's the point,' she argued. 'It's not your lawn. You might be willing to sacrifice a bit of grass and a few doors, if it means you can get Carnock because I'm too scared to stay.'

'I'll come back when you decide to apologise,' he said coldly, striding out of the kitchen.

Roxy ran upstairs and watched miserably out of the window as he began to herd the cows towards a gate she'd noticed at the far edge of the land. It looked as if the gate was open; someone had accidentally—or deliberately—opened it.

She made herself some supper, feeling dejected. Perhaps she was being paranoid. It could be a series of coincidences. Ethan and the men had found it really difficult persuading the heifers to move, despite the help of two sheepdogs. He looked very angry. Roxy decided she would give him the benefit of the doubt. She clambered out of the window and saw him coming over the terrace, a thunderous expression on his face.

'All right, all right,' she said, placating him with her hands. 'I apologise. I'm sorry. I was a fool and I admit it.'

He stared at her coldly. 'You have the nerve to own up?' he snapped, thrusting out his hand.

She looked at the tube of glue on his palm and raised questioning eyes to his.

'I found it in my car,' he said. 'The one you used.'

'How convenient,' she said tightly.

'Now you've just admitted——'

'I admitted I was a fool about thinking those enormous great cows were bulls, and that perhaps I was wrong to imagine I was being victimised,' she said hotly. 'Not that I engineered the whole thing.'

'But the top gate had been left open,' he said, a soft note of menace in his voice. 'No one around here would do that. Maybe you did it without thinking, but everyone living in the country knows it's vital to shut gates to keep stock from straying.'

'Oh, what's the use?' she cried in exasperation, turning away.

She was spun around, to meet his glittering eyes.

'I don't know what game you're playing, Roxy,' he grated, 'unless it's to make me feel sorry for you. That was quite a convincing performance out there—on a par with the one you gave as Seductive Siren and Cheeky Cockney.'

'No,' she protested, 'you're wrong. I couldn't make myself that frightened. You saw how terrified I was.'

'I almost did feel sorry,' he said. 'Hoping I'd comfort you?' His mouth twisted.

'You're disgusting!' she blazed.

'I don't think so,' he said silkily. 'You're a very responsive woman. You like sex, I can tell. It wouldn't surprise me if your devious mind had engineered this little scenario. You can act the fragile woman and I can act the protective male.'

'Don't be ridiculous,' she said levelly, meeting his hot eyes defiantly, miserable that he should think so badly of her.

'We'll conduct a little experiment, shall we?' he suggested. 'I'll kiss you, and you tell me you don't like it.'

'I can tell you that now,' she grated.

His fingers bit into her arms. 'Do it properly, Roxy,' he said harshly.

She lifted limpid eyes to his. There was a shadow around his eyes and he looked tired, but the green beam which came from them still managed to blind her with its brain-numbing power. Dizzily she felt herself tremble in his grip as he took one step to bring his hips against hers.

Reality was fast disappearing. Only the heat remained to fuse them together, loin to loin, and now breast to breast. Roxy felt a deep shudder run through Ethan's body, and then his mouth was moving against hers and she gave in to the now familiar sensation of losing control, drifting beautifully on the slow, sensuous tide of pleasure. But his teeth began to tug erotically on her lower lip and she surfaced, panicking.

'I don't want——'

He stopped her protest with a laugh that whispered into her parted lips and set her nerves dancing in delight.

'The hell you don't,' he muttered. 'Stop goading me, Roxy. Admit you like this.'

The remorseless head bent again and she clamped her teeth firmly together, fighting the urge to respond to him, gloriously, completely. There was a brief moment of relief when his mouth lifted and she was free from the relentless eroticism.

'I don't like it,' she whispered.

He smiled. His hands slid to her waist, and then jerked her top up, with a quick, experienced movement, his hands seeking possessively beneath the fine lace of her bra and easing it away with hasty fingers.

There was a flooding sensation of anger and desire inside her, an overwhelming ache. Moving slowly, like an automaton, she forced her reluctant hands to catch his wrists, but it was too late. His head had already bent and had found the rigid crest of her nipple, the totally unexpected sensation of his moist mouth tugging and sucking, unleashing a tide of torrid emotions which wouldn't be held back.

She groaned in her throat at the deep, throbbing ache within her. She felt the response of her body to his adoring mouth, and her nipple hardening eagerly, playing traitor too. It thrust boldly into his mouth, demanding that his teeth should graze it, that his tongue should slither sensually around it.

'Please——' she moaned, unsure of what she was asking for.

'I am,' he whispered into her throbbing nipple.

His fingers moved sweetly on its twin, and under the double assault she was helpless, her breathing as laboured as his.

'Ethan!' His name was dragged from her by his ravaging mouth.

'Tell me,' he coaxed. 'Tell me you like it.'

'Mmm, I do,' she moaned, quite mindless. She began to gasp out loud at the things his mouth and hands were doing to her, driving her crazy. 'Ethan, Ethan,' she groaned.

In the far distance a telephone rang, but they both ignored it, giving themselves totally to the hot, surging desire that possessed them both. But its insistence gradually penetrated their brains, and Ethan lifted his head from Roxy's swollen breasts, panting heavily. He stared at her, aghast, and she shut her eyes against the awful, damning truth: that she'd allowed him to touch her intimately, even though she knew he despised her.

White with humiliation, she pushed his shoulders and he moved back, abruptly.

'Why do I let you do this to me?' he said thickly.

It was useless to deny his accusation. He wouldn't face the fact that he'd driven her to this. Biting hard on her lip, she drew down her top, wincing as the soft material pulled against her tender nipples.

She flushed with embarrassment.

'Go and answer the damn phone,' he said in a savage tone.

In utter misery, she stumbled to the window and scrambled breathlessly in. She walked into the hall on leaden legs and picked up the phone, incapable of speaking into it.

'Hello? Hello? Ethan? Is that you, Ethan?'

'No. Roxy,' she managed.

'Oh, you,' said the voice rudely. 'It's Annabel Tremaine. I want Ethan.'

'You can have him!' cried Roxy.

CHAPTER SEVEN

FLINGING down the telephone, Roxy whirled around in a temper and stopped in her tracks. Ethan was staring at her in a very odd, thoughtful way.

'Your sister,' she snapped, indicating the phone.

His dark brows met. 'You didn't have to scream at her like a fishwife, did you?' His mouth an angry line, he picked up the receiver, covering it with his hand. 'You know she's not well. I won't have you upsetting her any more than you have already.'

'Why don't you both get out of my life?' she said coldly. 'And out of my house.'

He winced, then turned his attention to Annabel, whose voice could be heard, complaining. Roxy leant against the wall and folded her arms. She wasn't going to run away from him; this time she'd have it out with Ethan and demand that he went.

'Look,' he was saying gently, 'I had to get the heifers back. Now I need to board up a window. Eat your dinner and I'll put mine in the microwave when I get in. I'll be back as soon as I can.'

He made his goodbyes and Roxy wondered what was wrong with his sister that made him soften his voice in that protective way. She was shocked by the jealousy that pierced her breast. Nothing must make her forget that Ethan was sexually exciting but that that was the extent of his interest in her.

A liaison with him might be hot, sweet and passionate, but in the end they would part bitterly. That was how they seemed to be together: wanting and destroying, refusing to give an inch in the battle of the sexes. It was unlikely that he would show tenderness to any woman he conquered.

'You look as if you want to speak to me,' he said curtly, when he'd finished.

'After that disgusting assault, I want you to leave this house before tonight,' she said in an icy tone. 'I have no wish to be raped in my bed.'

He smiled in a calculating way. 'I'd never have to go that far, would I? You'd be panting for me long before I was that desperate.'

'I seem to recall you panting, while I admired a painting on the wall,' she answered coolly. 'The one with the small house in the corner and the tree to one side——'

'I know what you were doing,' he drawled. 'It's an ancient Chinese method of delaying a climax and prolonging pleasure.'

Her face grew pinched with outrage and she primmed her mouth. 'It's a modern English method of passing the time when you're bored,' she grated.

'Bored?' he queried, his eyebrow raised roguishly. 'I'll have to step up the stimulation next time.'

Roxy's will-power crushed the searing heat that coursed through her veins, determined to deny its presence.

'There won't be a "next time",' she said, lifting her chin in challenge. 'Because you won't ever set foot on Carnock land again. Ever.'

Anguish carved lines of pain in his face, and the barren bleakness of his eyes made her think of an empty, desolate sea. Her body fought her mind; she wanted to tell him the house was his, to say she wanted him to make love to her—anything, to alleviate his misery and the terrible knifing sympathy she felt for him.

Then his lashes dropped and he became as with-drawn and still as he had been on that fateful day when she'd first seen him, bare-headed and remote, filling her mind and soul and body with his image from that day, for every day. It was just as he'd sworn; there hadn't been a time when she didn't think of him. He occupied her thoughts relentlessly, remorselessly.

'Perhaps you're right,' he said quietly. 'It might be easier for both of us if I don't stay. I'll get my things. Do you think you can manage with the broken window? I'll send a man in the morning to board it for you.'

Trying to come to terms with the fact that he was really walking out of her life, Roxy didn't take in what he said about the window for a moment. Then she looked at him in alarm.

'You can't leave the place open to the four winds! What about burglars?'

Ethan pushed an exasperated hand through his hair, leaving it tousled and making her heart leap with an inexplicable longing.

'There doesn't seem to be any wind, it's not going to rain, and you'll be quite safe.'

'Supposing the Superglue people come back?' she cried, twisting her hands.

His cold eyes swept her body. 'All right. I'll board it now. My man will come in the morning to glaze it and I'll sort out someone to fix the doors. If you want to go out before they turn up, you'll have to open a window and climb out. If you have any trouble, my number is 543.'

'Thank you. I—I'm going to work in the study,' she said, unable to bear being near him. If she stayed she'd beg him not to go, and he'd treat her with such contempt that she'd never recover her self-respect again. 'Goodbye.'

A tense silence stretched between them as he studied her from under lowered brows. She was conscious of her own ragged breathing and the deep hurt inside her, hollowing her stomach and making her hands clammy. This could be the last time she saw him.

'Oh, will you *go*?' she cried, flinging up her hands as if to ward off the powerful magnetism that was drawing her towards him.

He gave a low laugh and obeyed.

Unable to contain her sense of frustration and chaotic emotions, Roxy strode up and down the study like a caged tiger, up and down, up and down . . . Her feet thudded heavily, her whole body trying to expunge Ethan Tremaine from her wretchedly infatuated mind and yearning body by forcing him out with every vigorous step.

Yet her ears were tuned to the sounds he was making as he boarded the window, listening for that moment when he'd walk across the terrace towards his car for the last time.

She flung her head back and groaned in rage. The man was destroying her. There came steps. She forced herself not to run to the window and watch him walk by. Then, with a despairing wail, she hurtled out of the study to the hall and hid behind the curtain, draped at the big full-length window beside the main front door.

His body was tight with temper, she saw as she peered around the curtain, unwilling for him to catch her spying on him. In fact, she'd thought he'd been making a lot of noise, hammering in the boards a few minutes earlier. It seemed a handful of nails had taken the brunt of his anger. They did seem to make each other *mad*!

He paused by the car, his broad back to her, allowing her a last lingering, admiring glance at the wide shoulders and tapering waist. Then, slowly, he turned, evidently reluctant to look at his beloved house for the last time, but incapable of leaving without imprinting it on his memory.

That was rather like her, she thought miserably, eagerly devouring every line of his body. She, too, was taking a last look at a loved... Roxy frowned. No! She didn't love him! It wasn't the same at all. Her heart began to thud as his head rose and he let his eyes drift up, over the façade of the house. And Roxy almost cried out aloud at the look on his face.

Never, in the whole of her life, had she seen anyone so haunted, so desperate. Imagining he was unobserved, Ethan Tremaine showed his depth of passion for the first time, holding back nothing. Before, she'd seen fire in his eyes, fury on his lips. This was more devastating to her heart, for her to see a strong, proud man look haggard and racked with despair.

She drew back, shaking, not wanting to see any more, and knowing she'd have to think very carefully about her motives for keeping the house from him. Perhaps she was wrong, she thought as she leaned weakly against the heavy curtain. Perhaps she ought to bow to the undeniable power of the generations and let a Tremaine return to Carnock House. The old lady might have had good reason to write Ethan out of her will, but what of the long term? What of posterity?

Suddenly Roxy didn't want a stranger in the house. If she returned to London and put it in the hands of an agent, how would she ensure that the buyer would care for the place, honour its commitments and spend the next few years replanting?

Anyone could buy it, she frowned resentfully. In the hands of an unfeeling, ignorant person it would be ruined, and she wasn't having that. She raised her head and smiled ruefully. After living here for five minutes, already she considered herself a country woman, with heart and soul devoted to Carnock! And... it was true, London seemed far away, further than a mere few hundred miles. It was another life, another, less attractive proposition.

In alarm, she checked herself. What was she saying? There was the business to cope with, the launch in Bristol... She groaned inwardly at the feeling of being enclosed and trapped. She didn't want to return. She didn't want to go back to being in an office and waking to the sound of BMWs leaving for the City, or the sound of clinking glasses on narrow balconies in the evening.

She didn't want to spend her life fighting her way through the rush hour, wheeling and dealing, ploughing her way through the mail, dictating, organising, cajoling.

Roxy's eyes widened at the discovery which hit with the force of a sledgehammer. She wanted to be here, in Cornwall. To smile at the pied wagtails as they ran over the lawn, their tails forever flicking up and down, their little bodies never still. To watch the sun set over the moor behind her lovely hills, to watch the fruit on the trees ripen and to wander barefoot through the warm grass. All that she wanted, with a deep yearning which permeated the whole of her being. Carnock.

And, she realised with a pang, she also wanted Ethan. The two went together, inseparable, filling her heart and mind to the exclusion of everything else. For complete happiness and contentment, she needed them both. Oh, what hell it was, to see your own paradise and not be able to enter it! Now she really knew how Ethan felt, banished from the place he loved.

The situation meant that her dreams were impossible to fulfil. There were only two solutions, and neither of them appealed. Either she could have Carnock—in which case she'd also have Ethan's enmity—or she could sell to him and know he was content—thus denying herself the two things she desired more than anything else in the world: Ethan and Carnock. What a choice. Would it be better to have neither, or one?

Gloom settled around her and the house seemed to grow sad, wrapping itself around her too, watchful and silent. Even with an extra jumper she felt cold, so she lit the fire. Outside it was pitch dark, the moon hidden tonight by thick cloud, moving swiftly under a strong wind. Owls hooted and she heard the scream of the vixen, loud and clear, then a cry which she now recognised as that of a Scops owl. She smiled faintly, soothed by the familiarity of the sounds. There was no fear in the night, now she knew something of its creatures and their habits.

A moth fluttered suddenly against the window and made her close the shutters so it wouldn't beat itself to death against the lighted window. Then the phone calls started.

The first time, she thought illogically that it might be Ethan, and she raced to answer, her heart pumping fast.

'Hello?' she said, trying to sound normal.

There was a nasty chuckle and someone began to pant. Cold ice touched her spine. She banged the phone down and stared at it. Someone has picked her number at random, she told herself. It rang again and her hands twisted nervously as she forced herself not to answer.

The third time, she picked it up gingerly, thinking it *could* be Joe, or someone trying to reach her, but the breathing began again.

'Who is this?' she cried, in panic. There was no answer. 'This isn't funny, just pathetic,' she snapped, and slammed the receiver down again.

It kept ringing. She almost disconnected it, but then she had an idea. She reached for her radio, selected an all-night channel playing pop music and set the volume as high as it would go. She lifted the receiver, listened for the breathing and put the phone against the loudspeaker, recoiling at the blast of sound.

She wasn't bothered again. Satisfied, she checked the windows were securely latched and prepared for bed. Snuggling down beneath the sheets, she reached out her hand to switch off the bedside light, then curled up, trying to block her mind and get some sleep.

When the doorbell rang, she heaved a huge sigh and rolled out of bed. She couldn't see Ethan's car outside, or anyone else's. It must be him; hardly anyone knew she was here, she reasoned, knotting the belt on her robe.

Perhaps he was hoping to catch her drowsy with sleep and persuade her to abandon her morals. He was very persistent. Warmth trickled into her veins and she bit her lip. Her will-power really was working overtime lately! Of course, she mused, she didn't have to answer. It was a pity her curiosity was so strong!

'All right, all right!' she cried, as the bell buzzed insistently. 'I'm coming.'

Roxy ran down the sweeping stairs, then stopped at the sound of another bell. Damn! He'd given up and gone around to the kitchen door. Roxy hurried along the corridor, expecting to see his big frame outlined against the panelled glass when she walked into the kitchen, but no one was there at all.

She heard a knocking sound. He was banging on the boarded window. No...the dining-room. Now the study...

A small prickle of fear chased up her spine and she felt the hairs on her neck rise. Her hand tried to rub away the chill at her nape as she followed Ethan's progress around the house by the four sinister knocks he made on every single window, pausing at the front door to press the bell again, and then continuing, right around the whole ground floor.

Roxy froze at the nasty chuckle. Maybe it wasn't Ethan.

In fact, she thought in alarm, it would be beneath his dignity to run around the house, ringing on bells and tapping on windows. Ice-cold sweat broke out on her forehead. She raised suddenly frail, helpless hands to press against her loudly crashing heart that seemed to thud in time with the rapid raps on each window.

Tap, tap, tap, tap. A pause. Tap, tap, tap, tap. A pause... Roxy could tell where the would-be intruder was by the sound and by the gap between knocks. Soon. She gasped in terror, willing her paralysed legs to move. He had nearly reached the kitchen, and when he rang the bell she'd see him, and he'd see her, in her brief nightwear.

Petrified, she stayed rooted to the spot, as in her rare childhood nightmares, when a witch had been coming towards her and she hadn't been able to budge an inch. But in her nightmares she'd forced herself awake and all that had been left was the memory of the sickening terror. This was real. There was no waking up, and she couldn't move.

Then slowly her heavy limbs obeyed her and she began to shuffle backwards, her terrified eyes fixed like saucers on the revealing glass in the kitchen door. She heard the knocking on the laundry-room window;

the kitchen door would be next. Her hand flew to her dry mouth, fingers plucking nervously at her pale lips. A dim shape appeared at the window and she screamed, soundlessly.

Yet it released her body from its numbing paralysis. Hardly able to control her violent shaking, she fled upstairs, moaning and panting in huge, choking gasps of breath. Beside herself with terror, she slammed the bedroom door shut behind her and locked it, frantically covering her ears so that she didn't hear the ghastly, frightening knocking. The front doorbell rang loudly and she jumped out of her skin.

Ethan—she'd ring him. Her shaking fingers hovered over the dial. Dammit! She couldn't remember the number! Rattled, she concentrated, disciplining herself harder than she'd ever done before. 543. Of course.

Almost weeping with relief, she tried to dial and found her fingers boneless from fear. She grabbed a pencil and jammed it into the numbers, listening in suspense to the ringing tone and willing Ethan to answer.

As she waited, she realised with a sudden jolt that the mysterious phone calls earlier could be linked with whoever was trying to frighten her tonight. And maybe the tractor, the cows, the glue...

Roxy's eyes darkened. Someone was trying to force her out. And, since he wasn't answering the phone, it could well be Ethan!

He'd threatened her before, sworn that he'd kill for possession of Carnock. Her hand dropped to her side, lifeless.

'Uh?'

Her eyes rounded, then joy surged into her heart. It wasn't him outside. He was at home. The sounds had stopped, but he obviously couldn't have made them.

'Ethan?' she quavered.

'Who is this?' came his sleepy gravel voice.

'It . . . it's Roxy,' she squeaked. Her heart thudded violently, but the fear was passing.

'What? It's gone two in the morning!' he grumbled.

'I'm frightened,' she said in a small voice.

'You ring me up to tell me that?'

'Oh, please listen!' she begged. 'Someone's trying to get in—they keep ringing the front door bell and the kitchen door one——'

'Tried opening them and saying hello?' he suggested sourly. 'This is the custom in these quaint parts.'

'Ethan, this is serious. He's been wandering about outside banging on the windows for ages and I'm locked in my bedroom petrified!'

She heard the receiver slam down and her mouth opened in dismay.

'You swine!' she seethed, glaring at the phone. 'You utter rat! You——'

The doorbell was ringing again. Furious now at having been left in the lurch, without any advice or comfort, she decided to take matters into her own hands. In the dark, she unlocked her bedroom door and tiptoed on to the landing, peering around the heavy damask curtain to the porch below. She was just in time to see a dark male figure disappear around the corner of the house, and immediately after, the tapping noises began on the windows again.

She could ring the police. Calculating it would take them at least a quarter of an hour to reach her, maybe twenty minutes, she discarded the idea. She might be raped and dead by the time they arrived. If only she'd had time to replace her alarm! That had worked well before. Her mind assessed the situation fast. So far, the Phantom Knocker hadn't broken in—and he could have come in through any of the windows if he'd really wanted to. That meant he *was* only trying to frighten her, not attack or harm her. Yet.

What she needed was to show him she wasn't scared and that she intended to defend her territory. Suddenly, she remembered the big earthenware jug in one of the bathrooms. Her eyes glinted with the light of battle as she hurried along the corridor. It seemed to take ages, filling the jug with water, and carrying it to the landing, but eventually she'd managed to stand it by the window which looked down on the front door.

The man would be round the back now. Carefully, as quietly as possible, she opened the window. After a few moments, she heard the man making his way to the front. Her stomach somersaulted. He was standing directly beneath the window.

With a strength born from fear, she bent down, picked up the heavy jug and emptied its contents over him, slamming the window and closing the catch in satisfaction. Now she'd ring the police.

In the background, she could hear the man shouting and she smiled coldly. On the brink of lifting the phone, she stopped. He was calling her name.

'Roxy! Let me in, damn you, Roxy!'

Ethan! Relief made her weak for a moment and then she was galvanised into action, leaping down the stairs two at a time.

'Stupid woman!' he was shouting. Roxy hesitated, frowning. 'Let me in at once! I'm freezing!'

Confused, she tried to work out what had happened, then the truth dawned. She'd drenched Ethan Tremaine! Aghast, she listened for a moment to his swearing, and then cautiously opened the door.

'About time,' he roared, pushing past her.

'Ethan! I thought you were the Phantom Knocker,' she moaned.

He was stripping off his soaking shirt, shedding water all over the hall carpet and treating Roxy to a colourful range of language, glaring at her balefully.

'Oh, dear,' she said, as Ethan's body shook and shivered. 'I think you'd better come into the kitchen. The stove's on. It'll be warmer.'

She led the way, apprehensively listening to the sound of squelching shoes behind her and Ethan's grumbles. Without a word to her, he accepted a towel and rubbed vigorously at his dripping hair. Roxy felt like a guilty schoolgirl at the way she was being studiously ignored.

'I'll put the kettle on and make you a hot drink,' she mumbled.

The light made his wet, bare chest gleam. Her eyes strayed sideways to the flexed muscles on his arms as he sawed the towel across his back. And then she discovered he was scowling at her ferociously.

'It was an accident!' she explained. 'I couldn't help it. I thought you were the man who was annoying me. You'd banged the phone down without a word and I thought you'd gone back to sleep in a huff.' His steely gaze made her falter. 'I—I didn't hear your car.'

'I left it at the barns,' he said tersely. 'In case you were telling the truth. I wanted to catch the intruder red-handed.'

'Well, I wasn't to know that,' she said stubbornly. 'When you arrived, you didn't yell out and say it was you. I wasn't expecting you to arrive. What did you expect? A brass band and fireworks to welcome you?'

'I expected a cowering, frightened woman,' he grated. 'Not a spirited and accurate defence, consisting of a cascade of iced water.'

'I nearly made it hot,' she admitted. 'Like boiling oil hurtling down from castle battlements. You ought to be glad it wasn't.'

'Glad?' His teeth were chattering and he clenched his jaw to control them. 'Suddenly I should be grateful to you for thoughtfully deciding to freeze and drown me, instead of scald me to death?'

Roxy blushed and became very conscious of her bare legs as Ethan stopped wielding the towel for a moment and took in their smooth length.

A tremor curled in a fascinating journey from her throat to her stomach. And then, as his gaze slowly wandered upwards, the coils increased and multiplied, wending their way down to her loins, settling there and shooting disconcerting charges of electricity in all directions.

He felt the same, she knew. The situation was inflammatory enough for any red-blooded man: the middle of the night, an isolated house, the two of them half-dressed. But it was potentially dynamite with an undeniable, if unwanted, attraction between them.

The atmosphere thickened, shortening Roxy's breath. Ethan looked imposing, stripped to the waist. His strong head and neck rose proudly from a powerful torso, and Roxy felt an unbearable ache to stroke its hills, planes and valleys. Men's bodies had never particularly enthralled her before, but Ethan's seemed to have been made for her eyes alone, the way it delighted her senses.

His waist was narrow, curving in from the broad chest that rose now with a huge inhalation of breath, the gleaming gold skin tantalising Roxy with its satin sheen. Her fingers fluttered, wanting to touch.

'Roxy,' he said thickly.

CHAPTER EIGHT

HER startled blue eyes blinked at the carnality in his expression, and she cast around frantically for something to say.

'You'll be warm in a minute. I'll find you a sheet and you can go home and we can go to bed—no, I mean you can go to bed in your home and I can——'

He gave a faint smile of understanding. 'Roxy,' he murmured, 'haven't you forgotten something?'

She frowned and thrust her hands through her dishevelled hair. 'I have?'

'The intruder?' he asked softly.

'Oh! Yes! That something! Well, he must have gone now,' she said lamely.

'That's convenient.'

She looked up sharply, and her lips parted gently at Ethan's intense gaze and sensual expression. He deliberately dropped his lashes, sweeping her barely clad body mockingly.

She moistened her dry mouth and his eyes narrowed in a calculating way. 'Convenient?' she croaked, her pulses hammering hard.

Ethan wanted her, and she didn't know what she was going to do. Her conscience told her that she must send him home with a flea in his ear and a selection of scathing words. Her body was fighting that idea, crying out for her surrender. At the moment her body was winning, hands down.

'Yes. *Was* there a man?' he asked in a soft voice. 'I didn't see or hear anyone.'

'Of course there was! I'd had some heavy breathing phone calls earlier, too.'

'Heavy breathing?'

He didn't sound in the least bit sympathetic or believing. Roxy flushed.

'Yes,' she said doggedly. 'Nasty chuckles, lots of hot panting. I didn't make it up! Why should I?'

'To get me here,' he said, watching her reaction intently.

'Why...' She swallowed. 'Why should I want to get you here?' she asked in a high tone, that sounded false even to her ears. She knew what he was getting at, but hoped she was wrong.

'Either to drown me, or to seduce me. I tend to go for the second reason, myself.'

Roxy gasped. 'You arrogant, self-opinionated man! You certainly get to the point without dressing up your words. Cancel the hot drink,' she said tightly, snatching away the towel. 'You can go home. And if I'm found dead in the morning, murdered in my bed, you'll only have yourself to blame.'

Her lips trembled, almost, she thought crossly, in time with her hands. If Ethan left, she'd be alone again and the man might still be lurking around. Her legs gave way and she dropped into a chair.

'You are frightened, aren't you?'

'Yes, I am,' she said shakily. 'Petrified.'

'Because you're spending the night alone for a change?' he asked, his tone hard with scorn.

'I must have been mad to call you for help,' she cried in angry frustration. 'There *was* someone outside, I saw him. I suppose you'll be telling me there are ghosts here. I'm not afraid of them, only hulking great bullies who enjoy breathing heavily down phones and trying to batter down my doors and break my windows. At least I have the satisfaction of knowing he's probably deaf in one ear.'

Ethan sighed. 'I'm going to regret this, but why might he be deaf?'

'The last time he rang and began to pant in that evil way, I treated him to a high-volume rendering of Michael Jackson's *Thriller* from my radio. I shouldn't think that did much for his ear-drums,' she said, her mouth curving at the memory.

He allowed himself a small grin. 'Now that is convincing. All right, I believe you. It all seemed rather unlikely. We don't go in for that kind of thing around here—with it being so tucked away, burglars and would-be rapists tend not to know the house exists. I rarely bother to lock up at night.'

'You're not a five-foot-four brunette,' she said wryly.

'You'd noticed?' he asked, a dangerous look in his eyes. 'Progress at last. Or are you going to throw me out now the intruder has presumably gone?'

This was awkward. He'd misinterpret any request for him to stay. Yet she was frightened and didn't want to be alone. Roxy brightened. There was a way out.

'I'd like you to hang on for ten minutes or so while I dress,' she said evenly. 'I think I'll try to find a hotel or something.'

'Don't be stupid,' he said curtly. 'You won't at this time of night. Oh, hell! I suppose you'd better come home with me.'

'No, thank you,' she said stiffly. 'I wouldn't presume——'

'Do as you're told,' he snapped. 'And hurry. It would be nice to get a little sleep before the dawn chorus. And I want to get out of these wet trousers before any frogs take up residence.'

He folded his arms belligerently and she saw that his mind was made up. 'If you're sure...'

'Roxy,' he said quietly, 'there's only one alternative, and that is for me to remove my trousers here and now, so they can dry in the airing cupboard. And you know what that means, don't you?'

She nodded. 'You'd get cold legs,' she said solemnly.

Ethan's huge slashing grin lit his eyes. And hers. 'Go and dress, woman, before I decide to make it perfectly clear to you what would really happen. Unless, of course, you're deliberately provoking me?'

'No,' she denied, backing out of the door. 'Stay there. I'll be down in a few minutes.'

'If you're not, I'll assume you want me to come and get you,' he murmured silkily.

She fled. Breathless with haste, she tore off her robe and nightie and scrambled into a soft wool skirt and jumper, thrusting a few things into a small bag.

'I've peered out of the windows, and it looks as if someone has been walking about on the flower-beds,' he said, when she came down.

Roxy clutched at her heart as it thudded wildly. 'Why?' she asked, her eyes wide in fear. 'Why would anyone act so bizarrely?'

'Come on. I want to get home. I don't expect it'll happen again. Someone's idea of a practical joke,' he said impatiently.

Ethan preceded her outside and held open the car door for her, and thoughtfully she wriggled into the seat, wondering at his shuttered face. She was reluctant to leave, and didn't know what she'd do the next night, but realised she didn't want to be alone. It was awful, being so dependent on Ethan. Maybe she should have contacted the local police station.

A soft buzzing puzzled her, until Ethan reached down and picked up a phone. While a woman spoke to him in a high-pitched and querulous voice, Roxy felt her face grow cold. He could have been the Phantom Knocker if he had a car phone! Was it possible that he'd tried to frighten her away from Carnock? And was that why he'd taken the full force of the big jug of water—because he and only he had been outside?

'I want to go indoors,' she said impulsively, tugging at his arm.

He frowned. 'I'm not here for your convenience— no, not you, Annabel,' he cried in exasperation. 'I'm talking to Roxy.'

He banged the phone down and drove off, his expression so intimidating that Roxy didn't speak again. But she worried. Somehow she must find out if he was guilty or not. It would make all the difference to the way she felt about him. Even her treacherously eager body wouldn't respond to a man who was hell-bent on terrifying the life out of her, for his own gain.

It wasn't very far to his house, the driveway being only a couple of fields away from Carnock's entrance gates. Although Tremaine House was so near, it had none of Carnock's atmosphere and she could see immediately why Ethan preferred his first home.

The farmhouse was large and very modern, built as if Ethan's father hardly cared much about the way it looked, but wanted a roof over his head and nothing else. The thing which struck her most forcibly was how immaculate it was everywhere, as if no one lived there at all.

Roxy half expected to see Annabel waiting for them, but the house was in darkness apart from one light upstairs. Ethan showed her into the square hall and flooded it with bright light, giving her a glimpse of the rooms which opened off it. While Ethan removed his shoes and socks, unwilling no doubt to squelch over the pale oatmeal carpet, she tried to gain an impression of Annabel's tastes—and his.

To her disappointment, it was difficult to come to any conclusions, except that the style had obviously been put together by an interior designer. From what she could see, it was well fitted out and full of smart, muted, colour-co-ordinated rooms which looked as if people rarely entered them, let alone curled up on a sofa with a bag of crisps, or sprawled on the floor surrounded by the Sunday papers. Shabby as Carnock was, she preferred its homeliness to this cool, impersonal remoteness.

'Come upstairs,' ordered Ethan curtly. 'I'm not opening my house for inspection this month.'

Roxy followed him, her eyes on his rigid spine. 'House,' he'd said, not 'home'. She tried not to feel sorry for him.

'Since I don't have a servants' garret, you can have a guest-room,' he said sardonically, not bothering to lower his voice.

'Don't you care if you wake your sister or not?' she asked, as he moved around the pristine bedroom, opening a window and making a fair amount of noise.

'She sleeps badly. Besides, I'm popping in to see her in a moment,' he muttered. 'Breakfast at seven sharp,' he added. 'Then we talk.'

'But——'

'We talk,' he grated.

He left her and she listened miserably to the sound of a shower running. A door slammed and there came the unmistakable rise of angry voices. Ethan seemed to be shouting at Annabel and she was protesting. How awful. Roxy had evidence now that he wasn't kind to his sister, after all. The row was awful and she felt embarrassed.

Were they arguing about her? Was it because Ethan had brought her here? Her face became concerned. He seemed to be giving his sister a piece of his mind. The noise died down and she tried to settle, but it seemed she tossed and turned constantly, trying to decide whether it really had been Ethan who'd tried to terrify her, or someone unknown. What would be worse? She wasn't too sure.

Then she remembered; he knew she'd been frightened by would-be intruders before, in London! Roxy sat up, suddenly wide awake. The swine! Incapable of remaining still, she got out of bed and walked up and down. It was probably part of his campaign to unnerve her and turn her into a gibbering wreck. Well, now she knew it was him, she wouldn't be afraid again.

With a groan, Roxy realised that she was now well and truly awake. Moving as quietly as possible, she went downstairs, hoping to make herself a drink to help her sleep. But she stopped in the kitchen doorway, disconcerted, when she found Ethan sitting at the big melamine-topped table, a mug in his hand, looking at her as if she was the last person on earth he wanted to see.

'Have you any hot chocolate?' she asked defiantly.

A jerk of his head indicated a cupboard. Roxy got herself organised and waited for the kettle to boil while the temperature inside her body rose higher and higher. Ethan wore a short white silk robe which clung to his body so lovingly that it was obvious he was naked beneath. And he was very tanned. Very masculine. Very...

Roxy gulped. Without lifting her eyes from the muscular bulge of his powerful, naked thigh, she knew he was watching her. Nervously she dropped a spoon, and quite thoughtlessly bent to pick it up. She should have left it where it was. For as her fingers touched it she heard him gasp, and her eyes shot up to meet his to discover that he was staring as if mesmerised at the deep swell of her breasts which her robe had failed to cover.

Dry-mouthed, she stayed immobile while he lazily surveyed the rest of her. A sensual curl tilted his mouth and his eyes grew a little glazed with desire. Roxy began to move—but too late.

Ethan had reached down and scooped her up, dropping her bodily on to his lap. His mouth clamped down on hers in fierce possession, obliterating any protest and almost her senses. But she hung on grimly to the edge of reality as his thighs burned their heat into her body and his hand slid seductively over her heaving breasts. Then she began to struggle desperately before the pleasure of his touch overcame her mind.

He laughed softly into her mouth and rose, dumping her unceremoniously on to the chair.

'Don't you like the way I treat you?' he snarled.

She shook her head, fingering her bruised lips.

'Then keep out of my way,' he bit. 'Stop flaunting yourself in front of me. I'm a man, not one of your city yuppies. Take that as a warning. I'm fully aware of your schemes.'

Not trusting herself to speak, Roxy let her face fall into a glacial expression and proudly tilted up her chin, then made her drink and strolled out with as much dignity as she could muster. She was convinced now that Ethan was no gentleman and capable of almost anything. He'd stop at nothing to get his damn house back, frightening her, bullying her, undermining her confidence.

She lay in bed, cold and miserable, wishing she'd never set eyes on him. He had such a mastery of her physical self, and was slowly taking over her emotions as well. Her life seemed to be dominated by Ethan Tremaine, she thought gloomily. Everything that happened to her, everything she did, seemed to lead to him. And she couldn't imagine what it would be like without him.

Lonely. Empty. That was why she hadn't wanted to return to London. Ethan wouldn't be there. Hostile or seductive, he was hooking her, fascinating her, working on the strong physical reaction between them to crush her.

Roxy gave a troubled sigh. If she returned to London, she'd never see him again. A sudden agonising pain seared her body, and her eyes opened wide in shock. If only there was someone she could confide in! Someone she could tell the truth to. She needed her mother. Oh, how badly she needed her mother!

To her consternation, her eyes filled with tears and she began to cry as if she'd never stop.

Her sobs rent her body so violently that she didn't hear someone come in. It was only when she turned into Ethan's arms that she knew he was there, and she flailed frantically at him, till she realised he was only holding her, nothing more, and murmuring soothing words. Besides, it was what she wanted. Tender, loving care. That was what it felt like, even if it wasn't intended, and Roxy shut her mind to anything else.

After a while he lay beside her, outside the bed-clothes, while she clung helplessly to him, able to speak a little at last.

'I m-m-m-miss my mother!' she sobbed. 'I w-w-want her b-back! I wasn't flaunting—and I don't m-mean to be a nuisance.'

'OK, OK. But you have to watch what you do when men like me are around. You can't act as if I'm one of your maiden aunts.'

'I d-d-don't have a m-maiden aunt!' she wailed.

He let her cry on, gently stroking her hair, occasionally wiping her face where the hot tears ran. Suddenly it seemed to Roxy that his face was very tender as he looked down on her, and that brought a fresh burst of crying. That died away eventually, too, and she lay in his arms weakly.

'This is awful. How feeble. I hate to be so pathetic. I haven't cried like this since I was a child,' she said, shamefacedly when she'd regained some of her composure.

'Everyone must grieve. It sounds as if you hadn't done so for your mother,' he said gently into her ear.

She turned her head on the pillow and he smiled at her. 'You hate me,' she said uncertainly, wondering why he'd been so supportive.

'Yes, and no,' he said wryly.

Her heart lurched crazily at the way he stared into her eyes.

'Ethan——'

'If you're feeling better, I think I ought to take you home. It's six o'clock,' he said slowly.

Her expression was crestfallen. 'Yes, of course,' she breathed. Neither of them moved. 'If only...' she began.

'Yes. If only,' he agreed, quietly, his steady eyes melting.

Her teeth bit at her lower lip. She wanted him to stay with her, but nothing would induce her to tell him that.

His hand lifted to push away a strand of hair from her forehead, and then one finger dropped to trace a small tear that oozed down the side of her nose. As if hypnotised by it, he leaned forwards and tasted the salt on her skin, and Roxy gave a small gasp as her treacherous breath refused to stay in her throat.

Slowly, Ethan's tongue licked the line of her jaw and her body awoke. Roxy touched his face with a wondering hand, and then they had moved together as if gliding through water, their kisses delicate and exploring as if they were both afraid of breaking the spell that bound them.

Mindless now, she let herself drown with him, helping him to remove the blankets between them and then her own nightclothes; her body a liquid heat against his. It was so natural that Roxy knew their fusion was inevitable.

Sweetly, every touch and every second of their journey a slow magic, they caressed each other, and for the first time Roxy knew what it was like to be adored, inch by inch, kiss by kiss. She felt the pressure of his mouth on every pore. His questing tongue invaded each hollow, his teeth gently nibbled each rise. Her skin tingled in anticipation as his worshipping head bent to a new place; her head thundered with wonder at the incredible sensuality of their actions.

She dared to explore his body, released by his own lack of inhibition and the total concentration of his lovemaking. Eventually she knew he was only just keeping himself under control and they parted, trembling with the intensity of their need.

'Oh, Roxy,' he groaned. 'Why the hell do I want you? Why does it have to be you who destroys all my good intentions and makes my body grow weak?'

His words reached to the centre of her body. He felt the same: powerless to deny the chemistry between them. Perhaps the only way they could escape the hold they had on one another was to give in and let their physical needs have full rein, until they were sated with each other and Ethan was ready to move on to another challenge.

That was all she was, to him, she realised sadly. The lure of the forbidden.

'It's your arrogance,' she said quietly. 'You refuse to let anyone beat you at anything, especially a woman. You hate the fact that I don't let you walk all over me, and you are determined to punish me for inheriting Carnock. I know what you'll do. Force me to submit, then boast about me to everyone, so that I'm embarrassed every time I go into the village.'

'Haven't my kisses told you anything?' he asked, hurt.

'Yes. You're an expert. It takes practice to be as perfect as you.'

'Perfect?' he smiled wickedly.

'No, I mean, I could see that any other woman would think—I mean, I don't, I—you see——'

'Roxy, you make me perfect. We are perfect together. You know that. When we make love——'

'There's no "when", Ethan,' she said coldly. 'I have no intention of giving you *carte blanche* to blacken my reputation and sneer at me.'

He frowned. 'Why don't you trust me? Why have you formed this warped and utterly wrong opinion of me?'

'My mother said——'

'Then she was wrong!' he said vehemently. 'I'm sorry, Roxy, I don't want to hurt you, but she seems to have made a lot of problems for us. I think it's time I cleared up one or two facts. But first, I want to tell you something.' He moved away from her. 'And I want to speak to you while I'm sober, not aching to make love to you, not in the heat of desire.'

Roxy stilled. Her eyes searched his, bewildered. Shaking his head, he rose from the bed, wrapping a sheet around his beautiful body. She tried to force her mind to come down to earth as he paced up and down, suddenly tense and self-contained. He was trying to forget her, trying to shut her out. No doubt he reckoned he'd been enticed.

'You think I'm cheap, don't you?' she whispered in a low tone. 'But I'm not, I've never been casual about love. Even now——' She bit her lip. She'd said too much.

Ethan stopped dead. 'Even now?' he asked gently. When she refused to continue, he came to sit on the bed beside her. 'Roxy, I don't usually risk exposing my emotions to someone I don't know very well. I'm too wary of being hurt. My trust in other people is not high, from painful experience. However intimately we have touched, our knowledge of each other is limited.'

She despaired. He was right. And their knowledge of each other had been limited to the carnal. How shaming. Now he was going to say something brutal—ask for sex without any strings, perhaps. Roxy waited for him to continue, in an agony of suspense. How easily she could be put through hell.

Her body had known the truth before she had, and therefore had been prepared to surrender; it had taken a little longer for her conscious mind to catch on. Roxy looked into Ethan's liquid green eyes and longed to be reckless. At that moment, it didn't matter what he wanted ultimately, or what he felt about her; she needed him. To her, he was the reason for her existence, her life-force. She loved Ethan.

CHAPTER NINE

'I'M NOT going to make love to you,' Ethan said unexpectedly, startling Roxy.

'I could have told you that,' she said with asperity.

What was he up to? He was slowly destroying her. Was that his punishment? He'd wanted her, she knew. It seemed his vengeance was greater than his desire. Ethan Tremaine was intending to smash her pride and self-respect, whatever the cost to his own needs.

'It's for both our sakes,' he said in a gentle voice. Roxy glared at its smooth charm and fixed him with cold eyes. His pretence of smug purity infuriated her.

'You don't trust me, I know, but listen,' he continued. 'I'm keeping my distance because I don't want you to think I'm using what I say to seduce you.'

'Really?' she asked in a bored tone. 'Forgive me, Ethan, if I'm a little confused——'

'You should try wearing my mind for a while,' he said ruefully. 'Roxy, you must be aware that I've been obsessed by you for some time, ever since you flew into your shop like a living whirlwind. Even your deceit was more amusing than I cared to admit. I wanted to laugh, and yet I hated why you were doing it.'

'I didn't know about the will then,' she said. 'You must believe me.'

'It doesn't matter. Nothing in the past does. In you, I saw more life and capacity for joy than anyone I'd ever known, and I envied that. I coveted it. I wanted you. When I knew who you were, I was more than disappointed, I felt devastated and I tried to make

131

myself hate you. Through a trick of bad luck, we've been cast on opposite sides. It's an obstacle I mean to remove.'

'And how do you plan to do that?' she asked, miserably. He'd set out from the beginning to trap her with the delights of his body, riding roughshod over her emotions so that he could *own* her. He'd hungered for her like a rich man after a beautiful painting, jealous of any other bidder. She shuddered.

'It's inevitable, isn't it, Roxy? We belong together, complete each other. You sense that, I know. Marry me.'

'Marry?'

She clutched at the sheet feverishly, twisting it in her hands. Ethan looked so stern, so incredibly reasonable, as if this was the most sensible solution he could come up with. He'd acknowledged the magnetism that drew them together, weighed that up against losing Carnock, and decided he could easily have both the house and his current passion.

Bitterness lanced in sickening spurts in her stomach, making her feel physically ill.

'Why not?' he murmured.

Roxy shut her eyes to his lying lips, wondering how long this unbearable misery would last. In her dreams she'd never envisaged Ethan asking her to marry him, nor had she believed that the answer springing to her lips would be a refusal.

'I mean to have you,' he continued, his voice very husky. 'Everything I want——'

'Oh, yes,' she said coldly. 'A woman in your bed to satisfy your raging lust and save you the effort of going out to find sleeping partners, and, by a pure chance, you'll have the one great love of your life.'

'I didn't know you realised,' he said quietly.

'You made it perfectly obvious,' she snapped. That house was his passion! Its attractions far outweighed those of any woman. Ethan's desire for Carnock burned deep. He'd even stoop to marriage if it meant acquiring his ancestral home.

Ethan looked puzzled. 'Don't you share that love?' he asked in a whisper.

She snorted, too miserable and angry to answer. It didn't matter what she felt about Carnock. It was their relationship which was the issue.

'Now we've established the advantages for you, what's in it for me?' she asked harshly. 'What will I get out of this arrangement?'

Ethan recoiled, not expecting her less than joyous response, and that gave her some small consolation. If she was hurting, then she wanted him to hurt, too.

'I thought—Roxy, I honestly believed——'

He searched for any sign of weakness, and Roxy steeled herself against the yearning within her, showing him only a woman who despised him utterly.

'You thought your seduction would be so wonderful that I'd want to fall into bed with you whenever you asked,' she said scornfully. 'You imagined you could have Carnock by offering me marriage. Well, it won't work.'

'It would,' he said softly. 'I'd make it work, even without love. What we have is an overwhelming passion. Many marriages have been based on less.'

'When I marry, I want it to be for love,' she said haughtily.

'That's what we all want, in our dreams,' he said tightly. 'But it isn't always possible. People can't love each other to order, can they?'

Her eyes darkened with pain. 'No,' she mumbled. 'I've learnt that, at least.'

'Try it,' he urged, his hands searching for her. Roxy's eyes glazed. 'You'd enjoy our nights together. I can guarantee that. Sex will be good between us, Roxy. You need me as much as I need you. I could make you forget everything in my arms.'

Yes, she thought, feeling herself swaying to the rhythm of his relentlessly seductive fingers and desire-filled eyes.

'No,' she said, shaking her head and compressing her lips tightly.

'When I touch you, we both light up,' he breathed.

'Not true,' she denied, shaking at his husky growl.

Ethan's fingers stroked her shoulder, kneading it gently, and it was all she could do not to fling her head back and let a deep groan escape.

'You're as crazy for me as I am for you,' he whispered, kissing her throat. 'I can offer you pleasure and the satisfaction of the hunger which rages within you.'

'There is no hunger——'

'Then why are your breasts begging for my touch?' he asked thickly. 'Why is your body hot and fevered?' His hands roamed her back. 'I said I wouldn't use the forces which draw us together, but I can't let you lie to me. I know you don't like the idea of giving in to your needs, Roxy, but why fight them?'

The deep pressure of his fingers on the taut muscles of her back made them relax. With that easing of her body began to flow her doubts. Did it matter if he didn't love her? He might learn, in time. She moaned as he pushed her back on to the pillows.

'That's it,' he coaxed, his mouth hot and demanding on hers.

'Don't touch me!' she hurled at him, as his hands slid to her breasts. 'I hate you, I hate you!'

'Not true,' he mocked. 'Your body is telling me something quite different.' His fingers stroked each nipple and they flowered for him.

'You're degrading me,' she whispered, trying to stop him from shaming her. But he ignored her protests and his mouth closed on hers, draining her of the ability to do anything but cling helplessly to him.

'I want you so much,' he groaned. 'Let me love you. Now.' His hands coaxed up her flimsy top, trying to remove it, then he caught his breath in passion and his lips were teasing the curving mounds of her breasts before she could stop him. 'You're so beautiful,' he growled, nibbling in gentle savagery. 'Give in. You know you want to. We have a lot to give each other.'

'What?' she husked.

A small impatient frown drew his brows into a brief line. 'Well, I will satisfy you, utterly, by making love to you as often as you want,' he breathed. 'You'll have my protection, if I live with you. And my expertise. I'd run the estate——'

That wasn't enough for Roxy. She wanted to be loved, really loved, not taken on as second fiddle to a house.

'No,' she whispered, her face white. 'Never! I wouldn't let you marry me, not in a million years. I'm going to put the house on the market and find a suitable buyer, and I'm returning to London this week. I want to get you and this sinister place out of my mind.'

The wind outside began to howl, startling them both. Ethan rose, and treated her to one of his basilisk stares. He cared nothing for her, otherwise he wouldn't have suggested such a cold-blooded proposition. Marriage without love was a living death to someone like her. Whatever she did, she mustn't waver. She was almost tempted to take second-best and accept, so much did she want to live with him. But she would be so miserable in the long run. Better to get it over with now and let the misery run its course. In a hundred years she might feel better, she thought wanly.

'I didn't expect you to refuse,' he said through clenched teeth.

He was angry, of course; furious at being turned down.

'You tried hard, I'll give you that,' she muttered. 'It's a pity you didn't take my personal distaste for you into account; you could have saved yourself the trouble.'

'Wayward and contrary,' he growled. 'Blowing hot and cold. So, I've made a fool of myself over you.'

She shrugged. 'We all do that at one time or another.'

He winced. 'It's over, then.'

That was that, thought Roxy, her eyes lowered. He was giving up. Depressed, she knew she had to hold on to her sanity until they'd parted.

'There was never really anything there, Ethan,' she said sharply. 'Only in your imagination.'

'Your body——'

Roxy realised she couldn't deny her physical response to him. 'Oh, that,' she dismissed scornfully. 'It's a long time since a man has shared my bed. But I don't need to marry you to remedy that problem, nor do I need to pay for my pleasure with a valuable house. You're good, I'll admit that, but I'd hardly say you were worth exchanging for Carnock.'

Ethan had stiffened like a ramrod, his face shuttered and grey.

'Leave this house,' he breathed. 'Go back to your city with its city morals and heartlessness. I want nothing of yours. Nothing at all. It's daylight outside.

It'll be safe for you to go home. I don't think your intruder will be waiting.'

'Neither do I,' she said coldly, certain that it had been Ethan. Her pulses raced as he appeared to be leaving her without a farewell. She couldn't bear that. 'Goodbye, Ethan,' she whispered, incapable of keeping her voice steady.

Still wrapped only in the sheet, he paused in the doorway, his back to her, then drew in a deep breath and took a step forward, as if to go.

'No goodbye?' she asked in an unnaturally high tone.

'What do you expect?' he snarled. 'A brass band and fireworks?'

Roxy's pupils became pinpoints of pain as her words were flung back at her vindictively.

'You don't have much of a heart inside that beautiful body, do you?' he grated. He threw her a savage look over his shoulder. 'Well, I have news for you. Neither have I in mine, not any longer. I'll get that house if it's the last thing I do. It's all I have left,' he added softly to himself.

'You have no legal grounds to claim Carnock——'

'There are ways,' he said darkly. 'More ways than you know.'

'Am I to expect a combine harvester to run me down in the lane? Ferocious dogs to pin me against the house? Tin tacks in the drive instead of glue on the doors, and you flitting around in a white sheet, pretending to be a ghost?' Roxy's eyes glittered angrily, remembering how frightened she'd been by his underhand tricks.

Ethan flushed bright red and all her suspicions were confirmed.

'You worm!' she scathed. Disappointment ran through her that he should have been so petty-minded.

'I suppose I'd better escort you home,' he said quietly.

'No. I don't want you near me,' she snapped.

Deliberately she turned her back on him and, after a few long, interminable seconds, he left.

Alone, Roxy wondered how happiness could change to such utter dejection in such a short time. He'd never loved her, never given a damn.

Her last sight of Ethan would be burned into her memory forever as he disappeared. There had been faint red marks on his back where she'd dug her nails in, in mindless passion. His dark head had refused to turn so that he could look her in the eyes, whereas he'd spent ages earlier just doing that.

And the deep huskiness in his voice had remained, but had become tinged with hatred. Mechanically Roxy dressed and walked out of the house, turning left in the direction of Carnock, weeping uncontrollably.

A gale was blowing and battered her listless body. With every step it seemed the wind grew fiercer, till she had to bend against it as she struggled down the drive, sobbing her heart out.

It was the end of a lifetime. Nothing in the future could be of any interest or pleasure. There was only bleakness, drudgery, isolation. She'd return to work and bury herself in it, becoming rich and miserable, bitter and lonely. And she'd never trust a man again.

Beneath the evergreen oaks it was shadowy, and she felt nervous as they creaked and complained in the wind. Instead of continuing around the sweeping curve of tarmac which led to the house, she decided to take a short cut across the lawn and get indoors as fast as possible.

She wanted a hot shower, to wash Ethan Tremaine out of her body. Then she'd ring for a taxi and catch the plane at Plymouth airport. The flight would only take an hour. Soon she'd be far from the man who had torn her life in two and tried to destroy her, all for the sake of Carnock.

Roxy's heart ached. A huge lump hurt her throat and the gale was lashing her salty eyes, whipping away the tears almost instantly. When the house came into sight, a pang assailed her.

Damn you, Ethan Tremaine, she moaned to herself. Seeing the big white building only intensified her anguish. This was where she wanted to live. For some inexplicable reason, Carnock was balm to her soul. Now, because of Ethan, even that had been denied to her.

It seemed like divine justice. She hadn't really deserved the house in the first place. Now Fate was ensuring that she learnt that lesson in the cruellest possible way. Suddenly she felt tired, and unable to stand the cut and thrust of life any longer.

Roxy reached out and laid her head wearily against the huge old redwood, feeling its fibrous, deeply divided bark. The wind blew her hair back from her face in a stream of dark tangles and she could hardly get her breath. But she welcomed it. Gust after gust caught at her, threatening to bowl her across the lawn, but she hung on, comforted by the strength of the tree.

All of a sudden, there was a tremendous crashing noise and she looked up in alarm, seeing an enormous branch tear away. She tried to run, but her legs would only move in slow motion. The wind tossed her off balance, and as she staggered she felt the crack of the branch as it hit her defenceless back and head. A beautiful, black, velvet silence swept all her unhappiness away.

There were voices, dim lights, and an odd muskiness. She felt terribly cold. Then she opened her heavy eyes to a narrow slit and found herself on the ground, the long painted nails of a tiny female hand beside her. Horrified at her nightmare, she tried to sit up, but slipped back into the welcoming darkness again.

'Roxy. Roxy.'

She turned, fretfully, not wanting to leave her lovely dream. She was blissfully married, to the man she loved, someone…someone… A deep furrow creased her brow. Who? Who was the man? He became hazy, indistinct.

'Roxy.'

'No,' she mumbled. 'Don't want to wake up.'

'You must!' breathed the persistent voice, far back in her head.

For a long while, she swam in the darkness and then a bright light shone in her eyes and she opened them in reluctance, her mouth pouting sulkily.

A man was smiling at her, his eyes a beautiful deep woodland green, and moist as if dew had fallen.

'Hello,' he said gently.

She stared at him blankly. He wore a face mask and a white coat, as if he was in a hospital. Cautiously, her eyes slanted around the room. It was a hospital.

'What's happening to me?' she cried in panic. Then, as she tried to move, she cried aloud in pain. It felt as if her back and head were as heavy as lead and being pounded by sledgehammers.

'Stay still,' said green-eyes anxiously.

'Are you a doctor?' she asked tremulously. 'Why am I in here? What's wrong with me?'

Her voice had risen in alarm, her fear fuelled by the dark-haired doctor's look of dismay. She lifted a hand to her head to find it was swathed in bandages. Mutely she blinked away the tears of self-pity which formed. Everything seemed to ache.

'It's all right. You had an accident,' he said slowly. 'Nothing broken, a few stitches in your head and a slight neck misalignment. A branch from a tree hit your head. You don't recall that?'

'No,' she whispered. 'When?'

'Almost two days ago,' he said, his face gentle. 'You were at home.'

'Home?'

She had the impression that he was looking at her keenly to see if she knew where 'home' was. However hard she tried, she couldn't summon up a picture, or a name. As for herself... Her eyes grew huge. She didn't know who she was, either. Her lips began to tremble and she raised piteous eyes to the doctor.

'Who am I?' she whispered. Her lids closed with the effort of thinking, and the lovely black cloak enfolded her again. Far in the distance, she heard the doctor's husky voice.

'Dear heaven!' he muttered.

The next time she came to, there was another doctor there, as well as the one with the lovely green eyes. He told her to relax and that she was in good hands, then asked her tiring questions.

She couldn't answer any of them. She had no idea what day it was, the month, the year, her name and age, or where she lived. She didn't know.

Aghast, she tried to delve into her brain and find the information for him, becoming more and more agitated as she discovered she couldn't answer what she knew to be simple questions.

All the time, her eyes kept straying to the green-eyed doctor, who looked as if he'd been on shift duty all night and was far too exhausted to be still working. His face was decidedly haggard and hollow-eyed, with a dark stubble curving around his strong jawline. He swayed on his feet and she couldn't understand why his soft grass-coloured eyes flinched every time she failed to answer.

She kept dropping off to sleep and they kept waking her, sometimes by lifting her on to an X-ray trolley, sometimes with more repetitive tests and the same questions. The weary doctor always stayed on the sidelines, watching. She began to smile at him, apologetically, every time she tried to guess the right answer and please the kindly doctor. Eventually, green-eyes decided to have a try.

'John, there's a possibility I might be able to help,' he said in an oddly husky voice. 'Let me do what we discussed.'

He nodded in agreement and turned to her.

'Now, don't worry about forgetting things. You're not special—it's not unusual,' he said. 'You realise your blow on the head has made you lose your memory, little lady?' She nodded slightly, wary of her pounding head. 'Temporary amnesia is quite common in cases like this. You'll probably remember everything in a few hours, maybe a few days, or it could take some weeks. The main thing is to let nature take its course. Aided, perhaps, by loving care,' he smiled.

She gave him a faltering smile back. 'Tell me who I am,' she whispered.

'Roxanne,' said green-eyes. 'Roxanne Page.'

'Doesn't sound like me,' she said miserably, her lashes spiky with tears.

'Roxy,' said the doctor in a gentle murmur.

'Roxy.' She sighed. 'It feels better—but strange. Who are you?'

He hesitated, then cleared his throat. 'Dr Ethan Tremaine. I'm an osteopath.'

'Do I know you?' She frowned. His eyes held some kind of message, but she couldn't make it out and that worried her.

'Am I familiar?' he asked quietly.

'I feel . . . at home with you,' she said lamely. That wasn't her feeling at all. His unusually powerful presence attracted her enormously. The fact that he was tired and overworked made her want to comfort him and help him to unwind.

'You've had enough to think about for now,' he said hoarsely. 'Dr White here has prescribed some tablets for you. I'll send the nurse in and she'll settle you down.'

'You'll be back?' she asked anxiously. He was her only contact, the only person she felt safe with.

'He's never left——' began Dr White.

'I'll be back,' said Dr Tremaine, interrupting his colleague abruptly.

Perhaps, thought Roxy, Dr White didn't want patients to know how overstretched the doctors were around here. The fact that Dr Tremaine hadn't been able to leave the hospital for some time didn't say much for their organisation.

Roxy let them make her comfortable, wincing as she tried to wriggle down into the bed. Her back was terribly stiff.

'I'll come and relieve those aching muscles of yours,' said Dr Tremaine gently, bending over her.

'I'd like that,' she murmured sleepily.

A flood of emotion rushed through her and she nearly put her arms around his neck. Horrified, she stared at him, her eyes clouding. She must be unbalanced if she felt like embracing a total stranger.

But the doctor smiled warmly and squeezed her hand which was clutching tightly at the sheet.

'Relax. Sleep is a good healer,' he said huskily.

The pills knocked her out for a long time. It must have been at least twenty-four hours, because Dr Tremaine was on duty again, looking as tired as ever.

'Hello, Doctor,' she said, ridiculously pleased to see him.

'Why don't you call me Ethan?' he asked. 'I'm going to be working fairly constantly on your spine, even after you go home.'

She beamed. 'I wonder if I've had a personal osteopath before?'

'Maybe this will bring back a memory or two,' he murmured.

He helped her to turn over and undid the ties on the hospital gown, exposing her back. Soon, his soothing hands were smoothing in a warm oil and Roxy felt her body relax completely.

'Lovely,' she murmured. 'Am I allowed to enjoy this? I want to make moaning noises but I'm not sure if that'll disconcert you.'

He chuckled. 'Oh, yes. All part of the healing treatment. Pleasure is to be encouraged. Well, Roxy,' he said, sliding his fingers up her spine and creating a melting of her bone and sinew, 'does this feel familiar?'

It did. Someone in the past had touched her like this. Her lover? Another doctor?

'I remember...' She blushed. 'Being touched.'

'Good,' he said throatily, and it seemed to Roxy that his voice vibrated through his fingers and deep into her body. 'That's a step on the way to recovery. Are you happier with your name today?'

'Mmm. Much. Do you know about me? Are there people worrying at home?' She had a sudden thought, and pulled her hand into sight, but there was nothing on her ring finger. 'I had a flash of memory then,' she said slowly. 'Something to do with marriage. But I'm not even engaged.'

Ethan Tremaine's hands stopped for a moment, then continued.

'No, you're not engaged. You have no relatives.'

'Tell me about myself,' she said dreamily, abandoning herself to his magical hands.

'I've been asked to let it come naturally to you as far as possible. We've done all we need, to keep your affairs straight. An old friend of yours is coming down in a couple of days, after you've gone home. He might jog your memory, if you haven't recovered it before then,' he reassured her.

'It's so awful,' she whispered. 'I feel so empty, so alone.' He didn't comment. Roxy felt disappointed and decided to say exactly what she felt. She was in hospital, after all. It was his job to care for her. 'I feel as if I've lost something more than my memory. As if I didn't enjoy my previous life, and couldn't care if I ever remembered anything again. It's such a void.

'I know what you mean,' he said, his fingers softly stroking. Roxy lay there tensely, finding his touch incredibly erotic. He was so good-looking, though, he must be used to stupidly drooling females. He spoke again. 'Many people would long to forget the past and wipe the slate clean. That's enough for now,' he added brusquely.

'I don't want you to stop,' she said with a sigh as he did up the cotton ties again. 'I love massage. It's heavenly. My headache is easier now. I'm sure if you'd gone on a bit longer, it would have gone away,' she said innocently.

'You've had enough,' he said sharply, lifting her back into a sitting position with surprising gentleness and strength. She felt immediately contrite. He was so busy, so harassed, and she'd begged him to prolong her treatment.

'Forgive me,' she said, touching his forearm and gazing earnestly into his face. 'You look as if you could do with a bit of relaxation yourself.'

He didn't answer, and his long black lashes prevented her from seeing any reaction. His face was very close to hers as he adjusted the pillows, and Roxy clenched her jaw at the overwhelming need to touch his smooth cheek with her lips.

'Ethan.' Had she said that, in a faint breath?

His hands stilled and he shot her a look from under his brows. Roxy saw the sultriness in his mouth and her lips parted in answer.

'I'll be back this afternoon,' he said coldly, straightening up.

Of course, she thought, as he strode quickly out. doctors had to be terribly careful about getting tied up with their patients. It was one of the hazards of the profession, she supposed, with half-dressed female patients feeling grateful and vulnerable, and male doctors looking dashing and protective.

A small memory nagged. Someone had offered to protect her. Why should she have needed that? Was she in danger? Or was she just one of those daffy women who couldn't cope without a man around? She certainly seemed to be acting stupidly as far as Ethan Tremaine was concerned, virtually throwing herself at him.

But he was rather gorgeous, and his hands didn't seem impersonal at all. Roxy lay enjoying the tingling

sensation on her skin. It felt invigorated. She felt...
A rueful smile played around her lips. She felt very
sexy.

There was more treatment from him. Each time he
called, he raised her pulse-rate. And soon she realised
he felt the same. Alarmed, Roxy knew that if he continued to treat her it would be only a matter of time
before he betrayed his Hippocratic oath. She mustn't
encourage him. Perhaps she could ask for another
doctor to treat her. Ethan Tremaine was far too
sensual in the way he looked at her, the way he moved,
in his husky voice and carved, kissable mouth. His
eyes entreated her, his fingers did their best to seduce
her. And she was falling helplessly for him.

CHAPTER TEN

AT FIRST Roxy was almost disappointed when she was told she could go home. Dr White explained her amnesia to her and said she must rest. Oddly enough, Ethan lived nearby, and offered to drive her back. A nurse had been engaged to settle her in—and it seemed she was wealthy enough to afford a housekeeper, too. Roxy found that odd. It was as if she'd always looked after herself and wasn't familiar with having other people around.

She and Ethan sat in the front of his car, the nurse riding in the back. It felt strange, driving along lanes she probably once knew like the back of her hand.

'Anything strike you as familiar?' asked Ethan casually, as they drove into a narrow lane.

She sighed and shook her head carefully. The headaches still caused her pain.

'Do I live in the country?' She eyed her clothes. They were rather gaudy and unsuitable.

'You live here.' He gestured to the driveway they were approaching.

'Carnock,' she read. 'That's familiar. Ethan, I recognise the name!' she cried eagerly.

'Gently.' His hand patted hers and then quickly withdrew at her wide-eyed look. 'How does it make you feel, the name of the house?'

'Happy,' she said decisively. 'Contented.'

She knew why, the minute they drove up outside the house. It was lovely. In a delighted daze, she wandered around, accompanied by the watchful and silent Ethan.

'I think you ought to go to bed now,' he said eventually.

'Not yet,' she begged him, turning around slowly. His eyes burned into her, sending a shock through her system. 'Ethan——'

'Don't,' he said huskily, shaking his head. 'You've no idea what you're doing.'

'I have,' she breathed. 'I know you, don't I? I can't feel like this about a stranger.'

'Yes. You knew me,' he answered quietly.

'Rather well?' she asked, holding her breath in anticipation.

He nodded slowly, but didn't move. Roxy realised he would never take the initiative; he couldn't while she was still his patient.

'I don't want you to see me in an official capacity again,' she said softly.

He winced. 'I understand.'

'No, you don't,' she said, walking up to him and laying her hands against his chest. 'Ethan, I want you to help me remember everything as a friend. Stay with me. Help me. You can't refuse. You're the only person I know who can put the pieces of my life together again.'

'Are you sure you want to?' he asked with a low growl.

'If my life contained you, yes,' she said simply.

'Oh, Roxy,' he groaned.

Now she was certain. They'd been lovers. From the way her body and heart leapt whenever he was near, and especially the way her skin tingled every time he touched her, she knew that they had been intimate. He'd probably been told to take things slowly as far as she was concerned. Well, she wanted to know about him. Everything.

'I'm a little weak-kneed,' she said truthfully. 'Help me into bed.'

'I'll get the nurse,' he muttered.

'Why?' she asked in surprise. 'You'd be much more able to carry me to my bedroom, wouldn't you?'

'If that's what you want,' he said, his lashes dropping to hide his eyes. He lifted her as if she weighed nothing. In his strong arms, she immediately felt at home and snuggled into him, lifting her arms to wrap around his neck. Her head tucked into his shoulder and she felt the rapid acceleration of his heartbeat.

Gently he placed her on the four-poster, which he'd said was her bed, but she wouldn't let go of his neck. Her eyes held his when he shot her a wary glance, and then, in a flash of recognition, she saw the love in his eyes and her face softened.

'Kiss me, Ethan,' she murmured, lifting her lips. 'I'm so confused and lost. I'm so in need of your kiss.'

With a stifled groan, his dark head bent lower and she closed her eyes as his mouth touched hers sweetly. Her hands twined in his hair, trapping him, and his kisses feathered in delicate, erotic movements over her entire face.

'Roxy,' he breathed. 'Oh, Roxy.'

'I knew what we felt about each other,' she breathed.

Reluctantly, he drew away, his strong fingers unlacing hers, and freeing himself.

'I shouldn't be doing this,' he began.

'Pleasure is good for me, you said.' She grinned wickedly.

His grin in return dazzled her. He was incredibly handsome, devastatingly sexy, she thought hazily. Her head throbbed and she pressed her hand against it quickly.

'Bad?' he murmured. At her little whine of agreement, he began to stroke her temples gently, then lightly massaged her neck.

'How clever of me,' she mumbled, feeling sleepy, 'to have an osteopath for my lover. You are my lover, aren't you?'

'Hush,' he whispered. 'We've both had enough discoveries for one day.'

'Stay till I fall asleep?' she asked, feeling her eyes close drowsily. 'It's nice having you around.'

He must have stayed, because when she woke he was still there, his face quite bearded. 'You have a visitor,' he said quietly.

Roxy's eyes followed his glance and saw a pleasant fair-haired young man sitting on the other side of the bed.

'Hi, Sleeping Beauty.' He grinned.

'Hi.' She smiled. 'Is this going to be Twenty Questions, or are you going to tell me who you are?'

'Joe,' he said gently. 'I brought you some flowers.'

'They're lovely, thank you,' she beamed. 'What incredible colours!' She wondered who'd put the clashing reds and purples with the garish orange.

'I knew you'd like them,' he said smugly. 'The florist was a bit horrified, but I explained that your colour sense wasn't like anyone else's.'

'I feel stupid, with you two knowing all about me and me not knowing anything at all,' she said sadly.

'Thank goodness for that,' grinned Joe. 'You've forgotten all my mistakes.'

'Mistakes?'

'Joe worked for you,' said Ethan.

'For me? Doing what?' she asked.

'We hadn't intended telling you, but the situation has become a little complicated,' said Joe. 'Ethan and I have had a chat and he reckons we ought to go ahead and fill in a few facts.'

Roxy listened in surprise as he told her of the company she owned. It seemed that there had been a takeover bid and a decision was needed.

'I don't feel well enough to handle it,' she said, worried.

'No one is asking you to,' said Ethan. 'The important thing is for you to get better. But I'm afraid only you can agree or refuse the bid.'

'What do you think, and Joe?' she asked. 'I need your help, you must see that. I can't think clearly at the moment. I trust you both.'

For a long time, they discussed the situation. Joe told her how much effort she'd put into the business, but she felt nothing for it now. It was in the past. The offer was good, and she would have the satisfaction of seeing the shops in major cities in the country—and a comfortable settlement.

'We think you should accept,' said Ethan. 'We went through all the possibilities and both came to the same conclusion. It'll be the best thing for you, for the company and the individual staff, especially as your enthusiasm seems to have waned.'

She gave a rueful smile. 'If you're right, Joe, that I tend to drop things I'm not fascinated by, then I can't see me running the business well. I honestly don't want to.'

'You want us to make the arrangements?' asked Joe.

She nodded. All she wanted was Ethan and to be at home.

Ethan rose. 'I'm going to ring Annabel and let her know you're staying, Joe. Excuse me, Roxy. I'll be back to give you a massage before I leave.'

Her eyes followed him to the last glimpse of his vented jacket.

'You love him very much, don't you?' observed Joe.

She gave a little laugh. 'Do I make myself that obvious?'

He nodded. 'He's crazy about you,' he said, delighting her. 'I think you'll be happier once you're both under the same roof. It seems he can't wait to ask you to marry him. I said he shouldn't hesitate, but he's not sure.'

'Because of my amnesia?' she asked.

'That's right. He thinks it isn't fair, that you ought to be in full possession of your senses. If you ever were!' Joe laughed.

'I have an idea that we had fun, working together,' she grinned. 'You won't lose your job with the takeover, will you?'

'No, there'll be an expansion, if anything. They liked the way I launched the Bristol branch you'd begun to organise. Well, I'll see about picking up my gear and bearding the dragon Annabel for supper. I'd much rather be here, eating with you, but Ethan said we had to let you rest. Mind you, I don't think he dares to be alone with you at night. He finds you far too enticing.'

She blushed. 'Tell me about Annabel. Who is she?'

'His sister. I met her when I arrived. I didn't like her much. She's got one of those pinched, mean faces. Her boyfriend is a nasty piece of work, too. Rather sullen.'

Roxy felt too happy to worry about a disgruntled sister. 'Come and see me before you go,' she smiled. 'And thanks for everything you've done.'

'Oh, anything for you, Roxy,' he said. 'Don't let Ethan slip through your fingers, now. He's perfect for you. A really nice bloke.'

Her eyes shone. 'I know,' she said. 'I'll do my best.'

Happily, she leant back on the pillows and waited for Ethan. The nurse came in to remove the bandage around her head on Dr White's instructions, and Roxy felt more feminine after the nurse had helped her to freshen up and change her nightie. Gently the nurse brushed her hair and teased it into wispy curls to frame her face. They were both satisfied with the result.

'I'll be off now,' said the nurse. 'Dr White says you can get up in the morning and he'll be along about coffee-time.'

'Thank you, very much,' replied Roxy, taking the nurse's hand. 'If you and Dr White and Dr Tremaine are anything to go by, that's a lovely hospital to feel ill in!'

'Well, it is, though it's a private nursing home, of course,' she replied. 'And strictly speaking, Dr Tremaine isn't on our panel. You're a lucky woman, to have a man so much in love with you as he is,' she confided. 'He probably won't tell you, but he never left your side and we had to force him to eat. He cancelled all his appointments to be with you.'

'What about his patients——?'

'Oh, he runs a huge practice. Dr Tremaine is renowned throughout Cornwall. He's trained up star pupils who took over his list—but none of them has his touch, of course. Now, I must go. You're in good hands, you know,' she added, with a laugh.

Roxy smiled. 'Yes. I realise that,' she said contentedly.

A little later, Ethan came in, and it seemed to her that he was adoring her with his eyes.

'Hold me for a moment, Ethan,' she pleaded. 'When I think what might have happened to me...'

'Sweetheart,' he muttered, sitting on the bed and taking her in his arms.

Roxy was content. His voice had been thick with emotion. He did love her. They stayed together for a long time, with Ethan gently stroking her hair. A deep peace settled on her mind. She raised her full lips and he kissed her tenderly.

'I love you,' she said simply, gazing into his eyes.

With an infinitely tender look, he lowered his head and kissed her again, and to Roxy it was the most fulfilling kiss she had ever known.

'I love you, too,' he husked.

The words ran through her body, warming every part, healing every wound.

'I've loved you forever,' she mused aloud.

He pushed her gently back. 'I have a guest. I don't want to leave Joe too long,' he said quietly.

'Joe. He's nice. But...I don't understand how I could run a business in London when I live here. The nurse told me we were in Cornwall.'

Ethan detached himself from her arms and stood up, his face oddly taut. 'It's a long story,' he said eventually. 'Too long for now. Goodnight, Roxy. I'll see you in the morning.'

He bent to kiss her and she pulled his head down harder on to her mouth. For a moment he resisted her little moans and whimpers, but seemed incapable of doing so for long and his kiss grew deeper and more passionate. Then, with an impatient mutter, he firmly prised away her fingers.

'I must go. Goodnight,' he whispered hoarsely.

That night she slept without the aid of pills and woke refreshed and ready to get up after breakfast, which Mrs Polruan, the housekeeper, brought to the bedroom.

Roxy had discovered that Mrs Polruan normally worked for Ethan, and she tried to prise more information from her. But the woman had been well primed and wouldn't discuss Ethan, nor the fact that Roxy had been living in her big house without anyone to help.

Gradually, over the next few days, the stiffness in her neck eased and the headaches came less frequently. She still couldn't remember the past, but didn't mind. The future was marvellous enough.

One warm, sunny May day on the terrace, they sat together on the teak bench. The shrubbery was ablaze with azaleas and rhododendrons, while the tall spikes of wild foxgloves rose thickly from an untamed area of grass. The air was filled with the sound of jackdaw chicks, demanding to be fed.

Ethan brought her some of the first strawberries in his garden, saying Annabel couldn't eat them.

Roxy thought it was a little odd that Annabel hadn't visited her.

When she mentioned this hesitantly, his arm tightened around her shoulder. 'Annabel rejects people, as my mother did,' he said quietly.

'Tell me,' she prompted, covering his hand with hers.

'She finds they don't live up to her impossible standards of hygiene and behaviour. It's an illness. And she's utterly selfish and can't see anyone else's needs at all. Mother, for instance, became neurotic and I was constantly in hot water.'

'In more ways than one, I suppose,' said Roxy with a faint smile. It can't have been easy, as a boy, living in the country, with a mother who wanted everything pristine.

'My life was a misery,' he said quietly. 'We tried to live with it, and Father was very gentle with her, but even he found her accusations and demands impossible eventually. They divorced and I lived with him.'

'They're both dead now?'

'Yes.' He met her eyes. 'Mother's funeral was on a rainy December day last year. I'd been trying to see her for some time, hoping to stop some evil gossip about me.'

'You mean she was spreading it?' asked Roxy, astonished. What an awful situation!

'Oh, for years she'd been making up stories about Father and me, the way we lived, the women who spent nights with us. The village loved it all, to think of orgies on their doorstep. Then Annabel decided to leave her, about seven years ago. It's difficult for two selfish people to live together. Mother saw that as a final act of treachery on my part—my revenge.'

'What did she do?'

'It tipped her over the edge,' he muttered. 'She took to her bed and never got up again. Next thing I knew, there was a story going around that I'd lured Annabel away to entertain my friends.'

Roxy's eyes showed her sympathy. Apart from the distress of the rumours, he must have been miserable that his mother felt like that about him—and that she was so ill.

'It got steadily worse,' he said bitterly. 'In the end, any last threads of love and pity had been cut away by her repeated phone calls and a flood of letters, all quite disgusting. She never forgave me for choosing Father. I belonged to her, she said. Now I have to keep an eye on Annabel, too. Her boyfriend is a psychiatrist and has been treating her. I can't say I notice much difference.'

'Poor woman,' sighed Roxy. 'Poor you.' With Annabel to think of, he wouldn't be contemplating marriage. Her face fell.

'Don't worry on my account,' he said, seeing her sadness. 'My back is broad. I'm used to Annabel. My method is to let her do what she likes with the house, and stay out as much as possible. It won't affect us.'

She turned her face up to him. 'Us?' she asked hopefully.

He drew in his breath and lightly touched her lips with his forefinger.

'I want to marry you,' he said softly. 'As soon as possible. I want to take care of you and love you like crazy, for the rest of our lives.'

Roxy's face lit with joy. Ethan loved her. She lifted up her arms to him.

'Hold me tightly,' she begged. 'I need you so badly!'

With a groan, he enfolded her in his safe, loving embrace.

'Let's marry now,' he urged. 'I can't wait any longer. Say you will.'

'Oh, yes, Ethan,' she murmured, delighting in his sweet kisses. 'But——'

He stiffened. 'But?' he asked, his face hard.

It frightened Roxy. There was a streak of steel running through him that she'd not seen before. 'I'm happy here, at Carnock,' she said hesitantly. 'I'm not sure I want to live anywhere else.'

He relaxed immediately. 'That's how I feel, too,' he said. 'Annabel can stay at Tremaine House and we can live here. I can keep an eye on her and maybe she'll marry her boyfriend. He's well suited to her.'

Roxy had the impression that Ethan didn't like the boyfriend, but she said nothing. She was happier than she could have believed possible.

'I want you to get better quickly,' whispered Ethan. 'I'm longing to make love to you. Desperate,' he said thickly, caressing her breast.

Roxy's body instantly responded and with a groan she clung to him. His eyes became as deep and as bottomless as the Pacific. She felt that she had launched herself into many men's eyes before and slipped out again with ease, whereas this time she was letting herself be shipwrecked willingly.

'I'm drowning,' she mumbled, amazed at the sensation.

He said nothing. But his mouth spoke to her in the way she wanted most. Hazily, with a mounting desire that increased with every breath, she watched the inexorable descent of his head. His arms tightened, so that she was crushed against his body. Then she felt the warm, soft flesh of his lips touching hers, sun-warmed, becoming hotter with their own internal flame.

His skin lay like smooth satin against her delicate face, and smelled faintly of soap. Her fingers lightly traced the jutting contours of his high cheekbones and slid down to his jaw, knowing they had all the time in the world to explore each other.

He shifted his body slightly and brought her hands down to slide within his shirt. Smiling into his kiss, and sighing in pleasure, she laid her palms flat, revelling in the slight give of flesh and muscle; the rocklike hardness of his chest.

A vision of Ethan like a granite rock, forbidding, inflexible and menacing, flashed through her head, and then was gone. He loved her. To reassure herself, she clung tightly, kissing him back with all her suppressed energy.

Ethan's breathing rasped in her ear, making her groan at its irregularity, and she twisted her hands in his soft, thick dark hair, urging his mouth to possess hers more fiercely. Encouraged, his hesitancy changed to passion and she was swept away by his ardour as his lips dropped hot kisses on her face and neck while she whimpered in her throat.

She became mindless, joy soaring inside her as his love devoured her, and she drifted on the flowing tides of sheer pleasure. A shudder ran through his body when he pushed up her T-shirt to cup her pulsing breasts. Kissing her throat savagely, he captured both surging, hard crests between his fingers, playing with them with such delicate skill that she could only moan in abandoned ecstasy.

Muttering hoarsely, he lifted her top higher and tenderly kissed the tight, sensitive peaks, then alternately caressed and kissed each breast until Roxy was gasping with need. Her skin was being stroked as if each fingertip adored her body, and her head dropped back in sheer animal pleasure.

'I want you,' he muttered hoarsely, covering her taut throat with kisses. She felt the harsh rasp of his tongue and intoxicating nibbles of her flesh as his mouth moved over every inch. 'Oh, Roxy!' he groaned.

'Ethan,' she whispered, in awe of her own feelings. A relentless throbbing drummed through her, making her body arch into his, demanding his hands, his mouth, his maleness. She was empty without him, inside her was nothing, and she knew that she needed him to fill her. Only his body and his love would pour life and substance back into her. It was the pagan need of a woman for a man, and only now did she understand its power and the overwhelming urge for union with someone you loved.

He bent his head to her breasts, suckling hard, and the sharp knives of arousal coursed like lightning through her body, searing it with white-hot fire and a startling electricity that created a wild physical energy within her. She reached out a shaking hand to smooth his dark head and looked down on his lowered lashes, lying thickly on his cheeks as his mouth sought to placate each demanding nipple.

And she urged him on, cupping the back of his head, begging him for more, till his frenzied mouth left two rigid, jutting peaks, moist and pulsating from his assault.

She could bear it no longer. 'I—want—you!' she jerked out.

Slowly, his hands still on her ribcage, he lifted his head. She saw hazily that his mouth trembled, full, still slightly pursed from encircling her tender nipple, his face was flushed with arousal and his eyes burned dark, the green obliterated by primitive need.

'I want you so violently that I'm in danger of hurting you. Stop me, Roxy. For pity's sake, stop me!' he said in a grating whisper.

In response, her body strained closer, refusing to be denied. Ethan groaned as her fingers gripped his shoulders, and her nails dug in. Somehow her mouth had nuzzled into his chest, kissing, slicking her tongue over the short dark hairs and seductively biting the firm flesh. A kick of excitement thrust deep within her when he quivered at her exploration. Her touch could excite him. Ethan seemed so experienced, so powerfully masculine. Dizzily, she raised her head, thrilled that his arousal could be increased by such a simple action.

'I'm almost . . . Roxy, I need you now! I did try to warn you,' he breathed. 'I'll try to be gentle, but . . .'

In defeat, he plundered her lips and her mouth became filled with his taste. The thrust of his tongue drove her beyond reason, past any inhibitions.

'Oh, yes,' she moaned, 'yes. Please, Ethan.'

'I'm drunk with your body, your eyes, your perfume. I want to devour you, to make you mine, to take you, over and over again,' he whispered harshly.

A primitive hunger lashed her with its fury, and with a swift, violent movement he caught her in his arms and lifted her up. The elemental fire devoured them as he strode unsteadily into the house, his teeth clenched for control, his thudding heart and pagan eyes betraying his need.

She turned her face into his neck and let the tip of her tongue drift over the silken, salty skin.

Ethan flinched and gave a small shudder. His heavy-lidded eyes were darkened and fever-lit, words of love tumbling from his lips in choking gasps. Roxy felt her own love rise up and claim her with its inescapable emotion, surrendering by letting her body melt into his, trying to tear off his shirt with frantic fingers.

He sank to the carpet with her, laying her down carefully, but she had the heat of desire within her and wouldn't let him be gentle. Her body shook with intense passion and at last, to her relief, he totally lost control. Her clothes were removed swiftly, easily, as if they were no barrier, and then he lay over her, flesh to flesh, branding her forever with his body.

'I love you,' he said thickly, arching over her.

Her heart lurched violently. She lifted her arms, mad with hunger, incapable of refusing him. His mouth crushed hers, deeply, probing, filling her with its fierce demand.

The sunlight shafted on to his high, angular cheekbones and she thought he was beautiful. 'Make love to me,' she croaked.

Ethan's breath drew in harshly. 'For a long time, I lived for this moment,' he whispered, hoarse with passion, caressing her breast. He kissed it possessively. 'Mine. To take possession. To have you loving me, stretched out like this...' She wriggled her body seductively, relishing his hot eyes, and he gasped in need. His hands ran down her curves in loving ownership and he smiled faintly. '...lying beneath me, naked, willing——'

The rest of his words spun into oblivion. Roxy's brain screamed in recognition. *Beneath me, naked and hungry.*

She knew who he was. She knew who she was. But, even though her mind had frozen, her body still reached for him as his fingers and lips aroused her, and she knew he was past sanity from the driving heat of his surging body. She would never stop him—nor did she want to. Roxy cried aloud in despair and longing at the hard thrust which joined them, knowing her treacherous flesh welcomed him and that it was sweetly easing his violation of her.

Ethan. Ethan Tremaine. Her enemy. She shuddered and his victory was complete as her desire overtook her totally, shattering her with the explosion that erupted within her, taken to incredible heights by Ethan's virile male power. The waves of pleasure rolled exquisitely through her, eradicating anything she'd known before, filling her with a sensation of completeness and wonder.

He was right, she thought wildly. They were wellmatched. He could satisfy her in a way she'd never dreamed. Every one of her muscles felt fluid. There was no pain in her body at all, only total release.

Yet in her head was the bitter taste that remained from loving Ethan and being used by him.

He had taken his revenge in the sweetest way possible. Crushing all resistance with his erotic, lying seduction, he had ensured her body would always cry out for him, even though her mind knew of his deceit.

Pleasure and warmth enfolded her flesh; a cruel knife viciously stabbed at her brain. Now she both hated and loved him, with a helplessness that made her want to weep.

CHAPTER ELEVEN

ROXY lay in utter despair, but too exhausted—physically, mentally and emotionally—to move. Ethan was murmuring lies into her ear and she squeezed her eyes shut so that the tears wouldn't come. Then she felt him hard within her again and grew cold with shock. Never again. She couldn't suffer a repeat of her humiliation.

'You're heavy,' she croaked, fighting the trembling of her body, as he caressed her thighs with tantalising fingers.

'Sorry, sweetheart,' he whispered, moving slightly. 'I feel like a triumphant victor.' He grinned lazily.

'I bet you do,' she muttered bitterly.

His body stopped its gently persuasive movement. 'What?' he asked, blinking as if to clear his head.

'Get off me,' she said coldly.

'Roxy——'

'I said, get off,' she grated through her teeth, fixing him with blazingly angry eyes.

'Darling——'

'Don't "darling" me,' she raged, pushing at his heavy body. 'My memory has returned. You've deceived me. *Get off!* I don't want you to touch me! I feel sick!'

Ethan lifted himself away, his face white. 'Not telling you we'd clashed at one stage was only a minor deception. You really loved me, so I didn't think——'

'You didn't think?' she repeated scornfully, snatching at her scattered clothes and dragging them on. 'Oh, you thought everything out very carefully. When you discovered I'd lost my memory, you must have thought it was your birthday! You deliberately set out to seduce me, in the same way you tried the first time we met. You can't deny that.'

'No, but——'

'*No!*' she yelled, making him wince. 'You wanted your damn house any way you could. If I wasn't going to give it up, you'd just have to take me as well. You lying rat! You fed me stories about your mother and mine—how dare you malign her memory? You got me in such a state that I thought I loved you. Well, Ethan Tremaine, you've lied and cheated your way into my bed, and I couldn't love you after that.'

'Roxy, you belong to me——' he began quietly, his eyes bleak.

'No, I don't!' she hurled. 'You took me. There's a difference. You had your revenge, I admit that. I did want you, and you succeeded in making me beg for you. But never again.' Her head lifted proudly and she looked down on his big, naked body in disdain. 'I'll have this carpet taken up and burnt,' she said with cold savagery. 'I'll wash every one of your fingerprints off my body, and it'll be as if we'd never touched.'

Ethan flinched as if she'd hit him. 'Not so,' he said hoarsely, green eyes glittering like hard emeralds. 'You'll never forget me. Moments like that, passions like that, are rare and unforgettable. You will need me, as I need you, Roxy. And when you've calmed down, I'll come and explain everything to you.'

'Don't bother,' she snapped.

'Your body will remember mine. My fingers on your body, the hammering of our hearts——'

'I'll remember nothing,' she lied, as the curls of desire pounded in her veins at the sultriness of his voice and the longing in his eyes. 'Only that you nearly married me. Another week or so and I would have been your wife! And Carnock would be yours again! Well, I'm keeping it. By persuading me to sell my shops, you've given me the money to stay. And no amount of threats, like nocturnal phone calls, will get me out.'

Ethan had begun to dress, and was fastening his belt. At her last defiant sentence, he grabbed her wrist, holding the delicate bones in a grip of steel.

'That wasn't me,' he growled. 'That was Annabel.'

'You liar!' she cried in a low voice. 'I saw a man outside. It was you. How could you put the blame on your sister?'

'I've kept quiet for too long,' he grated. 'You will listen to me.' He wrenched her against his body and pinned her arms behind her. She twisted her head away from his hot breath and bared teeth. 'Annabel has always wanted Tremaine House to herself,' he said. 'She cleans the whole house right through, every day, and I get in the way merely by being there. When I heard about your phone calls, I knew who it was. She was doing what my mother did—but persuaded her boyfriend to start a vendetta against you.'

'Why should he do anything so stupid, and why should she want me out of the house?' asked Roxy coldly.

'Because I could move in, of course. As for her boyfriend—well, I gather he was expecting her to inherit the whole estate from my mother. That's why she handed over the sealed will when she found it. If she'd known she wasn't mentioned, she'd never have owned up to having it. I had a row with her the night you stayed with us because you were frightened. She said her boyfriend wouldn't marry her unless she could offer him more than herself. He wants to give up psychiatry and become a gentleman farmer. With Tremaine House, that would be possible.'

'How did you manage to persuade the nursing home to let you seduce me, while I was lying helpless in bed?' she demanded, accepting his explanation but refusing to let him know that.

'Dr White knew my feelings about you. He thought I might be able to jog your memory,' he whispered through white lips.

'You calculating bastard!' she breathed.

He jerked her hands, pressing her against him. She gasped at the sheer physical elation which tried to melt her determination to resist him.

'You know you love me. You know you want me,' he muttered, his mouth sultry and hovering close to hers.

'I don't,' she bit. 'Your coarseness, your crude sexuality makes me ill.'

He released her suddenly and searched her face. She masked all her whirling emotions, making her expression cold and hostile. To her relief, Ethan stepped back, his mouth working, and obviously accepting what she said.

'You hate me,' he said hoarsely.

'That's the understatement of the century,' she said, her voice shaking with despair. If only she did. If only she didn't need him to complete her life. If only he wasn't such a single-minded swine who lacked any moral values at all.

'And you're staying in Carnock.'

She could barely hear him, he spoke so quietly. 'Yes. and you're going. Now. And you can tell your house-keeper not to bother coming in. I'll find someone of my own.' She folded her arms and faced him squarely.

'I won't give up,' he said. 'Not ever.'

'At the first sign of a campaign to get me out, I'm going to the police,' she said levelly.

'I wasn't thinking of the house,' he murmured.

Roxy shivered. He intended to make her admit she wanted him.

'You had me once. Let that be enough,' she said, trembling at the memory.

He smiled menacingly. 'It whetted my appetite,' he drawled, reaching for his shirt. 'As it did yours.'

She had to lick her dry lips before she spoke, her eyes hypnotised by the satin play of muscles on his chest as he slipped into the shirt.

'I'm finished with men,' she said shakily. 'I intend to devote my life to restoring this house and its grounds.'

'You'll be hungry soon,' he said with a mocking smile. 'And I'll be back, to take what's mine.'

He moved threateningly towards her and she backed away. The hard wall hit her spine and his hands splayed out on the wall on either side of her head. She knew his intention. It was below her dignity to struggle. She'd show him that his kiss did nothing to her.

His pelvis moulded perfectly to hers, declaring the extent of his arousal. His mouth twisted at her in-voluntary gasp and he took advantage of it, forcing her lips apart with his invading tongue, taking full possession of her mouth. His hands gripped her arms hard, biting into the flesh.

Roxy's body stayed rigid, her lips cold and un-moving. But her heart lurched in misery and she wondered why she had fallen for such a ruthless, heartless devil as Ethan Tremaine. If she allowed him to do this again, it would signal her own destruction. By denying herself, she'd live in perpetual misery. By giving in to her obsession for him, she'd condemn herself to total humiliation.

Eventually his calculated insult ended. 'Remember me, Roxy,' he whispered, one finger rubbing her nipple. To her dismay, it tightened immediately and he gave a grunt of satisfaction. 'Remember me,' he repeated. 'Soon you'll wish you'd never recovered from your amnesia. I intend you to beg for me. I'll accept nothing less from you.'

He turned on his heel and left. Roxy sank to the floor, utterly spent. He'd been so certain. In his hard face was only cold determination, a terrible vindictiveness in his eyes.

Oh, dear heaven! she moaned. How had she ever become drawn into his twisted life? All the Tremaines were evil. It was extraordinary that her mother had stayed for such a long time. Maybe if she discovered a little more about the family it would give her something to fight him with, if he ever turned up again.

Slowly she clambered to her feet. She was alone in the world. She had to pull herself together and make herself powerful. More important, she needed a manager to throw Ethan off her land if he ever dared to set foot on it again.

Roxy made herself a cup of coffee and drank it sitting on the grass, carefully avoiding the terrace where her seduction had begun.

There was a flash of black and white wings as a croaking magpie was chased low over the lawn by a soft grey collared dove protecting its nest. And almost immediately a small brown shape emerged from the bushes on her right, with six jackdaws in hot pursuit. As she watched them dive-bombing the stoat, jabbing it with their vicious beaks, she thought numbly that protection of 'home' was a deep-seated and instinctive reaction.

And, she sighed, so was mating. Yesterday she'd seen two slow worms entwined on a bed of moss. A bolt of desire plunged through her as her treacherous brain filled with the image of herself and Ethan, their naked limbs imprisoning each other.

Restless, she finished her coffee and jumped up, shutting him out of her mind. She had a great deal to do and no time to indulge in wishful thinking.

By the time the rhododendrons began to fade, and the jackdaw fledglings were trying to fly, Roxy had installed a manager in one of the cottages on her land and was reading everything she could lay her hands on to learn what she could about farming. During the days, she was far too busy to think about Ethan for long, since the house rang with the sound of decorators, furniture restorers, builders and furnishers, while the peace outside was shattered by the sound of tree surgeons rendering safe the old trees and the landscape designer arguing with her gardener.

Gradually she became involved with life in the nearby village. The school held its annual fête, and she contributed to the raffle with gift-wrapped items from 'Zest!', whose London office was run by Joe. She found life slow and easy, the people welcoming.

Only her nights were empty, and it was then that she yearned for Ethan with a deep passion that shook her. So she flung herself into even more frenzied ac-

tivity: entertaining, joining the village choir, the
Women's Institute, the library delivery service—anything to exhaust herself so she could sleep without
that deadly desire to be in Ethan's arms.

One of her proposed parties became the talk of the
village. It was to be held in the huge drawing-room
of Carnock House, the overflow being easily accom-
modated in the spacious hall. A firm of outside
caterers had prepared dishes from an old recipe book
she'd found, and everyone was to come in Georgian
costume.

She'd chosen a low-necked dress of flimsy white
muslin which floated beautifully around her body, and
had curled her hair around a pretty rolled band of
the same material. It was such a grand occasion that
for the first time she felt in need of a partner, to share
it with her, and greet her guests.

Roxy hid her tremor of longing behind a brittle
mask, her eyes bright with forced excitement and the
fortification of champagne. The chatter made her
head ache and she was trying to listen politely to the
gossip when she became aware that there was an icy
silence behind her.

She turned slowly, a premonition making her hands
sweat. Ethan stood just outside the drawing-room
door, a wide-eyed and frightened Annabel on his arm.

For a moment, she drank him in hungrily. His
proud, square head lifted in proud defiance, its lines
clean and as beautiful as ever, his eyes challenging
her. A deep, perfectly tied green cravat matched the
colour of those incomparable eyes, and the forest-
green Regency jacket made a sweeping curve over his
deep chest. The tight gold kid breeches hugged his
legs shockingly, and Roxy's eyes glazed.

He took a step forwards in the arrogantly black and masculine boots, and she knew the whole room was waiting, wondering how she would throw out the renegade who had the nerve to gatecrash her party.

But a flicker of movement drew her eyes away from him, and she saw how violently Annabel's hand was shaking. Roxy met his eyes steadily and glided forwards, holding his gaze.

'Good evening,' she said coolly.

A mocking smile twisted his lips. 'You know Annabel, of course,' he murmured.

'How do you do?' said Roxy, holding out an impersonal hand.

Annabel reluctantly drew her hand from Ethan's arm and let it lie limply in Roxy's. She looked down on the tiny, scarlet-tipped fingers, and her eyes widened in recognition. Annabel grabbed Ethan again and a musky perfume filled the air. There was no doubt: it had been Annabel by her side when she had lain semi-conscious under the redwood tree.

She froze, her smile fixed unconvincingly. 'Stay for a short time if you must,' she said. 'I don't want to make a scene for your sister's sake. But I choose who comes to my parties and I prefer not to pour champagne down the throat of the man I despise.'

Someone turned up the background music and a gang of young men began to roll up the Persian carpet as the laughing guests moved to one side. With a threatening look at Ethan from under her brows, Roxy slid into the arms of one of the young men and began to dance.

A succession of partners followed, each delighted with her sparkling gaiety, each holding her as if she were precious, an apparition likely to vanish, a piece of delicate china. And all the time she vehemently longed for someone to grasp her with hands of steel and force her body to move with his, to demand her submission.

Ethan, she noticed, as her laughing face scanned the room, had taken as many partners as she had. None of the young women seemed reluctant because of his reputation. In fact, they were positively eager, and to Roxy's fury he held them tightly, clasping them to him possessively, smiling down on them with a mixture of desire and mockery that made her heart wrench in sheer jealousy.

Swine! She would show him she didn't care. Deliberately she let her laughter peal out as her bemused partners tried to be witty. Encouraged, they let their hands wander a little, and it was all Roxy could do not to thrust them away.

A slow, moody melody drifted romantically over the crowded room, and someone turned off the main lights so the room was dimly lit. Roxy's body twisted with pain as Ethan's hands slid up his partner's back and began to massage her spine.

In an agony of envy, she moved her wooden body, every muscle tensing when Ethan's fingers strayed to the woman's hair and caressed the back of her neck. Strangely enough, she couldn't recall the woman at all. She must be the girlfriend of someone she knew. Her lips compressed into a thin, hard line. Ex-girlfriend. After Ethan's sensual touch, she would want him.

Roxy knew he was deliberately creating this scene. he'd promised she would beg for him. Her teeth ground together in fury that he was right. Inside, she was begging. But never in reality. Never, never, never.

The music ended and she made her escape after a brief thanks to her partner. She would slip outside for a dose of ice cold air and get some sense into her veins. Ethan, however, was too quick for her.

Before she knew what had happened, she was in his arms and moving to another, wickedly sensual tune, the husky-voiced singer echoing the low growl in Ethan's throat.

'Just keep your hands in the right places,' she warned him.

'Pity you didn't say that to your previous partners,' he replied, his eyes murderous.

She shot him a glance. Mercifully, there was a distance between their bodies and he couldn't know how hard her heart was beating.

'I enjoy being touched by some men,' she said sweetly, desperate to prove she had no desire for him. Only then might he leave her alone. 'My celibate days are over, you see. I began amusing myself to see if it was your devastating sensuality which had temporarily made me insane, or only a normal response to a starvation diet. I discovered,' she said, giving him a flirtatious tap on the lips with her finger, 'that it wasn't you at all! Now I'm fully integrated into the . . . er . . . community. Regularity is always so important for one's health, don't you think?' she asked lightly.

The grip on her hand tightened till she winced in pain. 'You slut!' whispered Ethan through tight lips. 'I should have known you had one hell of a past. No woman could respond with such eroticism to everything I did unless she'd been extensively tutored.'

She gave a tinkling laugh, trying to ignore her crushed hand and Ethan's menacing face. He was very possessive. And he hated the idea that she no longer wanted him. She *had* to keep up the pretence.

Her eyes fluttered at a group of young men as she fought to ignore the pulsing energy that forced her towards Ethan. He drew in his breath and pressed his hand hard in the small of her back, the meeting of their bodies sending shudders through both of them.

It's still there, she thought miserably, following the journey of the sensual power which travelled its relentless path within her. She felt her stomach muscles contract in dread as his thumb circled the inner flesh of her wrist with terrible effect.

'I want you,' he muttered.

His eyes were cruel, his smile mocking. It would be a battle for supremacy between them, then.

'Me? The house? Which would you choose, Ethan, if it had to be one or the other?' she asked with a cool smile.

'You.'

'Liar,' she said calmly.

The touch of his body was unbearable. Unlike her previous partners, she knew she was dancing with a man. He led her masterfully, making her dip and sway, and she knew they looked good together. A flush stole into her cheeks as his hard thighs angled against hers and the heat of his desire forced her to arch back, away from him. But he held her relentlessly, and through the thin fabric of her suddenly revealing dress she knew he could feel the burning in her own loins.

Still she kept the upper part of her body bent back, her spine straining with the effort. Something in his deep, husky breathing made her flick him a glance, and she was transfixed by the open carnality in the glittering green eyes.

They were freely roaming over her partially covered breasts, the filmy muslin drifting alluringly over her honey-gold curves, where her flesh swelled as if trying to entice him.

'Virginal white,' he growled sardonically. 'The ultimate lie.'

She couldn't tear her eyes away from his lusting face. Small movements of his hips tormented her beyond belief, insulting her, telling her that she was cheap and on offer to him as well as others.

The hands that held hers in an iron grip tucked in between their bodies, and Roxy grew rigid as his thumb stroked at her breast. To hide what was happening, in case anyone was looking, she jerked herself forwards, against him, and felt his big hand splay against her spine, so that she couldn't free herself.

He laughed softly, his thumb rotating without mercy, till she bit her lip to prevent herself from crying out.

'Don't,' she said desperately.

'Like it?' he drawled.

'No.'

'You silly fool. Why should we torture ourselves? Why let anything come between our physical need for each other?' he asked in a soft husky voice.

His breath feathered her forehead and she felt a gentle kiss land there, making her quiver with indignation.

'You hypocrite,' she whispered.

'At least I admit I hunger after you,' he said brutally. 'We're both highly sexed. Why shouldn't we satisfy each other? Do you really want to pretend to me that these boys can please you?'

'In sufficient numbers, yes,' she said daringly, too desperate to think straight and avoid danger.

'You bitch,' he breathed.

In a swift movement he had whisked her out of the drawing-room and, before she could open her mouth to protest, forced her into the study and slammed her against the door. Roxy opened her mouth to scream and it was filled with his hot, fiercely stabbing tongue, her instant reaction being to sink with a shuddering sigh into his arms as he locked the door behind her.

CHAPTER TWELVE

AFTER a second, Roxy regained her wits. Against his big, threatening body, she wriggled frantically, hating his domination and his short victory. She flinched as his mouth savoured the width of her jawbone and his hand dipped inside the flimsy material of her dress to raise her breast to his avid gaze.

Drawing a sobbing breath of outrage, she intended to yell, but her protest changed to a moan as his swift dark head bent to capture the throbbing globe with his relentless lips.

'Oh, no,' she groaned, gasping as languor promised to envelop her.

'Oh, yes,' he whispered. 'It's been a long time for me, and I'm not going to be thwarted.'

'Annabel's waiting for you,' she cried, through bruised lips.

'She's gone home.'

'That woman you fondled——'

'A friend.' His hands explored the jut of her hips. 'She helped me to set the trap.'

'Trap?' she husked.

'Mmm. To find out how jealous you might be,' he said laconically.

Roxy felt the hot colour flood her face, and saw to her embarrassment that the golden globe in his tormenting hand was stained with pink too.

'Interesting,' he mocked. 'I wonder if the rest of your body is blushing.'

'No——'

Too late: he had slid the dress from her body in one savage movement. Roxy felt limp with fear as the satin of her skin tingled from the force of the desire that flowed from him. She opened her mouth, no sound emerged. Mute, she stared at his heavy-lidded eyes in horror.

'Now,' he said thickly, his voice laced with desire, 'you might have spread your favours far and wide, in which case I'm claiming my turn.' His finger flicked her stomach insolently and trailed downwards. She flinched as his fist tangled in her dark hair, but still she couldn't move or speak, only gasp with shallow, harsh breath. 'Or,' he continued, 'you're trying to deny your need for me. Either way, you're getting me. And I'm taking you.'

'Ethan,' she croaked, 'don't treat me like this——'

'I'm in hell,' he growled. 'Why not you? I fill my life with work and it isn't enough. All I can think of, eat, drink, sleep, is you, you, *you*!'

Roxy moaned. So it was with her. How could they rid themselves of this destructive obsession? Maybe his way was the only one. They would grow tired of each other eventually. Ethan expelled air from his body in a harsh sound, and suddenly Roxy felt his warm mouth on her thighs, then, helpless to stop him as the cruel tyranny of need dominated her senses, his mouth searched the soft inner flesh and she rocked with the climax that rent her body.

Gently he lay her down and she heard him removing his clothes. He covered her and she muttered raggedly into his ear, begging him, as she had sworn not to, yet knowing that he was begging her, too, both of them incapable of holding back. Her legs wrapped around him and through veiled eyes she saw dark colour suffuse his skin.

'Roxy, Roxy,' he muttered brokenly, 'I love you. I can't live without you. Hell! There's no way I can convince you of that, only take what I know is mine.'

Her head reeling, she felt him raise himself a little, and forgot his words in the fierce intensity of his male thrust, matching his savage possession with a desperation of her own. In exultation, she cried his name, deep from inside her chest, melting sweetly like honey so that she flowed into him.

'I love you,' she whispered miserably, as they lay exhausted in a tangle of limbs. 'I wish I didn't.'

'It's taken you a long time to give in,' he said quietly.

She turned her head away from his piercing eyes, not wanting to see the cynicism there.

'I can't go on without you,' she mumbled, humiliated. 'I—I'd rather you were with me, even if I come second.'

'Second?' he murmured, kissing the edge of her mouth with great care. 'Sell the damn house. I'll still want you. I'll still love you. I can't bear to see you unhappy, Roxy. You're so stubborn. I had to make you admit what you felt. Come away with me. We'll live anywhere, providing we can be together.'

'You really mean that?' she asked in wonder, staring into his eyes. They weren't cynical at all. They were filled with anxiety. The breath caught in her throat as he nodded solemnly. 'I'll put it in the estate agent's hands in the morning,' she said, testing. He didn't even flinch.

'I wish you would,' he said passionately. 'Two misguided old ladies have cursed this place, as far as we're concerned.'

Roxy stiffened instantly at the slur on her mother's character.

'It's true, my darling,' said Ethan earnestly. 'I'll show you. Dress. Annabel has brought your mother's diary and my letters. She found them with the will when she plucked up courage to go into the dirty attic and clean up. When she read them, she realised...well, you'll see. For now, all I'll say is that she thought that, for her own purposes, it was better if she kept them. Seeing me so miserable about losing you, she changed her mind. Please. For the sake of our future, dress and come with me.'

Uncertainly Roxy let him lead her through the hall, where the party continued unabated, no one apparently noticing her absence. He collected a parcel, wrapped in gift paper and tied with a large bow.

'For you,' he said, his eyes serious. 'A gift from me to you, with my love, in the hope that you'll read every word and understand. Goodnight.'

Astonished, she accepted his kiss and watched him walk away, her eyes riveted to his broad shoulders in the dark green cloth. He didn't even turn, but reached the open front door and kept going into the black velvet June night.

Clutching the parcel, Roxy fled to the kitchen and with trembling fingers undid the ribbon.

For the next two hours she read, the noise of the party dying gradually till the house lay in silence. And finally she did understand.

Ethan's letters were a model of restraint, but she could read the heartache between the lines, and in his responses she knew what awful things his mother had accused him of. He'd returned some of her letters and they were still attached to his. Roxy felt ill when she read them. Mrs Tremaine was sick—the bitter accusations were far beyond those of a normal person.

From the way her own mother's diary read, Roxy could see how Mrs Tremaine's tales had gradually become convincing. At first, Milly Page's diary noted things the old lady had said: comments about Ethan's heartless rejection of his mother, the way he'd hastened his father's death by the orgiastic, drunken parties. Finally Roxy sadly read of her mother's indignation that her employer had been devastated by Ethan's calculated and vindictive efforts to lure Annabel away. It hadn't been like that at all. Her mother's sympathy had been misplaced. Worse still, it was obvious that she had spread the tales to people in the village. No wonder Ethan had been angry.

Aghast, she closed the diary. Milly Page and Mrs Tremaine had truly become embittered, their sense of judgement warped. How could her mother have been so blind? Roxy paced up and down, thinking. She was the kind of woman who never questioned her employer, who conformed, and regarded those she served as her 'betters'. Her mother had been at the beck and call of others for so long that she had forgotten how to think independently.

She had a kind heart and her caring nature had instinctively sought to protect the frail woman she worked for. Like birds protecting their young, she thought sadly. The constant grumbles from the old lady and the stories with elaborate detail had coloured both their lonely lives. They'd turned in on themselves to disastrous effect.

Roxy felt miserable to know her mother had hurt the man she loved, but she understood. And Ethan had seen Milly Page's interference, and had been refused admission to his mother's home so often, that he imagined she'd swung the will in her own favour. Roxy bit her lip. She had to tell Ethan he was wrong.

She rushed into the darkened hall and a figure detached itself from the shadows, making her cry in fear.

'It's only me,' said Ethan.

He stood with his hands thrust into the narrow pockets of his breeches, his legs straddled. But the pose wasn't arrogant, only speculative.

'I read the letters and the diary,' she said nervously, her fingers twisting and twining together. 'I see now what kind of woman your mother was, and that my mother never imagined Mrs Tremaine might be mistaken.'

'When Father and I left Carnock, and then finally Annabel left, there was little else for my mother to think about. Every hour of her day was spent in plotting, planning, hating,' he said quietly. 'Your mother was caught up in that. There was no proof—you don't need any, in a village environment. Word of mouth soon obliterates the need for that. Stories are carried and enlarged.'

'What are you going to do about your reputation?' she asked.

'Nothing. The stories are fading and in time will be forgotten.'

'I'm sure Mother didn't pressurise Mrs Tremaine to change her will——'

'I know,' he said gently. 'I thought that too. You could tell that from the way your mother wrote. She was absolutely honest. I was wrong and I'm sorry.'

'I'm sorry you've had such a terrible cross to bear,' she whispered. 'No wonder you were furious when you heard I'd inherited.'

He smiled faintly. 'I saw you as shallow, immoral, incapable of managing Carnock decently, and likely to paint each door a different shade of orange.'

She gave a shaky laugh. 'Is that all? You—you seemed keen to take advantage of me. Was that so you could manipulate me?'

'Nothing as dramatic,' he said softly. 'I was falling helplessly under your spell, and hated you for causing my insanity. I hated myself for giving in to it, and pretended I only wanted to seduce you to gain power over you. In reality, I couldn't keep my hands off you. You were untidy, a madly sophisticated woman and a spendthrift. I could see ruination for Carnock. And still I wanted you,' he growled.

'Tell me one thing,' she said, remembering, her hands clammy. 'What were Annabel and her boyfriend doing the night I was knocked out?'

'Oh, Roxy.' He came towards her and tipped up her chin, seeing her trembling lips and the damp eyes. He kissed each lid and licked away the tears which welled out. 'A branch did break off the tree and hit you. Annabel's boyfriend had been on his way to pester you again and found you lying on the ground. He did nothing, but went to fetch my sister. They could have left you there, and no one would have found you for days. Perhaps you would have died from exposure. But she sent him to ring for an ambulance and then to fetch me. She stayed with you, covering you with her cardigan.'

'She has a heart, then,' quavered Roxy.

'Yes. And when I told her what I felt about you, and that I wanted to marry you, she agreed to come with me to the party, knowing you would throw me out if I came alone.'

'Was it an awful effort for her?' asked Roxy sympathetically.

Ethan nodded. 'She's hardly seen anyone for months, apart from her boyfriend. But now she's sent him packing and wants us to help her brave the world again. What do you think?' he asked cautiously.

They stared at one another across the wide hallway. With a muffled cry, Roxy flew to him and he caught her fiercely. She buried her head in his shoulder, as he crushed the breath from her body for a few glorious seconds.

'I couldn't bear seeing those damned men pawing you,' he growled, when he let her surface. 'I wanted to fling them all through your drawing-room windows.'

'And I'd just had them re-glazed,' she chided.

'Did you hate it?' he asked hotly. 'Or did they...' His eyes became anguished. 'Did they excite you?' he asked in a hoarse whisper.

'Oh, no, Ethan!' she cried. 'They left me ice-cold, whereas you only had to scowl at me and I longed for you. I hated you for that,' she said huskily.

'We must start searching for another house in the morning, my darling,' he said, kissing her cheekbone, his mouth lingering. 'I don't think I can wait to marry you, and be your husband.'

Roxy's heart leapt crazily. 'You must love me very much to reject Carnock so definitely. I know what your passion was for this house,' she said softly.

'It's nothing to what I feel for you,' he whispered, tasting her ear. 'Wherever we go, we'll need a huge bed if I'm to give my passions their freedom.'

She was content. The solution that she had never thought possible was about to be realised. She felt smug. It was possible to have it all. Carnock and Ethan.

'I want to stay here,' she murmured, lifting her radiant face. 'Now I know there's no competition, and I come first.' She grinned. 'Flesh and blood is better than bricks and mortar, isn't it?' she asked, a wicked glint in her eyes as she wriggled seductively against his body.

Ethan grinned a little dazedly. He reached out and touched the wall behind him, his fingers moving over the beautiful panelling of the door. Then he touched her in the same way.

'Better,' he agreed, the light in his eyes both tender and brimming with desire. 'And now, I think, that flesh and blood must yield. If I'm to stay in Carnock, then we must begin to create the next generation to enjoy the trees we're intending to plant.'

'Yes, my lord,' she smiled teasingly, as his mouth hovered above hers. Her body moved provocatively, its sensuality for him and him alone.

This time would be like no other. It would obliterate the sorrows of the past, and give them the future they both dreamed of.

'Take me,' she begged. 'Possess me.'

'As you possess me,' murmured Ethan.

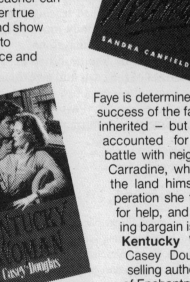

TASTY FOOD COMPETITION!

How would you like a years supply of Mills & Boon Romances ABSOLUTELY FREE? Well, you can win them! All you have to do is complete the word puzzle below and send it in to us by March. 31st. 1990. The first 5 correct entries picked out of the bag after that date will win **a years supply of Mills & Boon Romances** (*ten books every month - worth £162*) What could be easier?

```
H O L L A N D A I S E R
E Y E G G O W H A O H A
R S E E C L A I R U C T
B T K K A E T S I F I A
E E T I S M A L C F U T
U R C M T L H E E L Q O
G S I U T F O N O E D U
N H L S O T O N E F M I
I S R S O M A C W A A L
R I A E E T I R J A E L
E F G L L P T O T V R E
M O U S S E E O D O C P
```

CLAM	HOLLANDAISE	OYSTERS	SPICE
COD	JAM	PRAWN	STEAK
CREAM	LEEK	QUICHE	TART
ECLAIR	LEMON	RATATOUILLE	
EGG	MELON	RICE	
FISH	MERINGUE	RISOTTO	**PLEASE TURN**
GARLIC	MOUSSE	SALT	**OVER FOR**
HERB	MUSSELS	SOUFFLE	**DETAILS**
			ON HOW
			TO ENTER

HOW TO ENTER

All the words listed overleaf, below the word puzzle, are hidden in the grid. You can find them by reading the letters forward, backwards, up or down, or diagonally. When you find a word, circle it or put a line through it, the remaining letters (which you can read from left to right, from the top of the puzzle through to the bottom) will ask a romantic question.

After you have filled in all the words, don't forget to fill in your name and address in the space provided and pop this page in an envelope (you don't need a stamp) and post it today. Hurry - competition ends March 31st 1990.

Mills & Boon Competition,
FREEPOST,
P.O. Box 236,
Croydon,
Surrey. CR9 9EL
Only one entry per household

Hidden Question _____
_____

Name _____

Address _____
_____
_____
_____ Postcode _____

COMP 8